This book should be returned/renewed by the latest date shown above. Overdue items incur charges which prevent self-service renewals. Please contact the library.

Wandsworth Libraries
24 hour Renewal Hotline
01159 293388
www.wandsworth.gov.uk

THE BRIGHTER BOROUGH
Wandsworth

Also by Otto De Kat in English translation

A Figure in the Distance
Man on the Move
Julia
News from Berlin
The Longest Night

OTTO DE KAT

FREETOWN

Translated from the Dutch by
Laura Watkinson

MACLEHOSE PRESS
QUERCUS · LONDON

First published in the Dutch language as *Freetown*
by Uitgeverij G. A. van Oorschot, Amsterdam, in 2018
First published in Great Britain in 2020 by

MacLehose Press
An imprint of Quercus Publishing Ltd
Carmelite House
50 Victoria Embankment
London EC4Y 0DZ

An Hachette UK company

Copyright © 2018 by Otto de Kat
English translation copyright © 2020 by Laura Watkinson

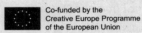

Co-funded by the
Creative Europe Programme
of the European Union

N ederlands
letterenfonds
**dutch foundation
for literature**

This publication has been funded with support from the European Commission. This
publication reflects the views only of the author, and the Commission cannot be held
responsible for any use which may be made of the information contained within.

This publication has been made possible with financial support from the
Dutch Foundation for Literature.

A CIP catalogue record for this book is available from the British Library.

ISBN (MMP) 978 1 52940 162 2
ISBN (Ebook) 978 1 52940 161 5

Part 1

1

Maria

"He was a Fula.

"I say 'was', because I haven't seen him for a long time. I don't know if he's still alive or, if so, where he might be. He just disappeared.

"He was like a son to me. Son – that's such a beautiful word, isn't it? A word with longing in it. As soon as I say it, I can see him walking up our drive, with a helmet on his head. It was just before Christmas and it was raining. Yes, I'll admit it sounds like the beginning of some old tearjerker.

"When I opened the door, there he was, a postcard in his hand, just waiting to be made redundant – hesitation from head to toe, no conviction at all: *We Wish You a Merry Christmas and a Happy New Year. From* Trouw *newspaper and your delivery person.*

"He handed it over saying a word. I couldn't see him too well. It was still dark, and the visor of his helmet had dropped halfway over his eyes. The black jacket and the black trousers didn't improve the situation. A Happy New Year – could there be any gloomier way to make that wish?

"I asked him if he wouldn't mind taking off his helmet for

a moment, to make it easier for me to talk to him. He did, and then I saw his face. Small and black, withdrawn, with eyes that did not look at me. Short curly hair.

"'You're always up and about early, aren't you? When there's hardly anyone else around,' I said. Something like that. The conversation didn't exactly flow, not that first time. He just nodded and gave me a hint of a smile. All that rain made it look more like crying. I gave him ten euros, and thanked him for delivering our newspaper.

"He stood there awkwardly holding the money, before stuffing it into his pocket, and then reached out both hands to shake mine. I told him to come back if he was ever out of work. And that maybe I could help him. I've often wondered why I said that."

"Not a single day has gone by when I haven't missed him, and it all started then. A dark-skinned boy, in a helmet, who grew up on the edge of the jungle, and somehow ended up in a backwater full of newspaper-reading affluence. Of course he didn't look at me. What he could see all around him was so unfamiliar.

"The sound of his voice when I asked him his name.

"'Ishmaël.' He pronounced it in a slightly nasal tone, with the pitch of a different continent.

"'You come back here, alright? If you ever need anything,' I said to him. What a strange thing to say. Who invites a young man, a complete stranger, to come to their house?

Was it impulsive? Prompted by some kind of embarrassment?

"And yet I meant what I said, without any doubt. Even though I'll admit the words took me by surprise. But it was more than a mere impulse. I know for certain that what I had said expressed what I felt.

"Looking back, I thought it must have been to do with the time of year. Christmas, about to embark upon a Happy New Year. Everything under control, and every year better than the last.

"That was almost eight years ago now. Eight years, seven of which were happy ones. Well, not all the time, of course – that would be impossible. But yes, I'll call them happy, because that's how it seems, looking back. Those were the years with Ishmaël, and when I think of Ishmaël it's as if someone switches on a light inside me."

"It's so kind of you, Vince, to agree to see me, and to listen to what I have to say. And what a good idea it was to go for a walk along the dyke. It's much easier to talk here, so much freer. I was scared you'd want to see me in your office at home and I wouldn't know what to say. But walking here with you, Vince, it helps me get my thoughts straight.

"Do you mind me telling you about Ishmaël? Yes, he is called Ishmaël. I feel like I've come to a dead end. I'm looking for a way through this, trying to understand what happened with him. Maybe you can make some sense of it, of what I want to tell you. You do specialise in other people's stories, after all. I'm hoping that maybe you can explain why he left."

"I live in a house that's set some way back from the road. You wouldn't know it. Maarten and I moved there about six years ago – you probably don't even know that. Thirty kilometres along the river and you're in a different area, with a new town where you go to do your shopping, and there's almost nothing to remind you of where you used to live.

"You have to follow a gravel lane to get to the house, more grass than gravel, with trees and bushes either side. The garden's pretty big, as my back kept telling me. I've stopped gardening now. I used to cope with the garden at our old place, but this one's intimidating. It's too much to handle."

"Ishmaël closed his visor and walked slowly into the rain. He had leaned his moped against the fence. I saw him climb onto it. I'd walked some of the way with him, an umbrella over my head, and stood watching him go. A short curve and he disappeared from sight. I knew I was never going to see him again, and the thought made me a little sad.

"But then, with a longer curve, he reappeared, three months later. It was cold, the end of March, winter was over, but spring had not yet really begun. A dead time, when everything is waiting.

"I was working in the shed, stacking kindling wood, or something like that, when I saw him standing at the end of the drive. He didn't move or dare to enter the garden without being invited. I waved at him to come on in, and then walked over there, since he still had not moved. Feeling a little awkward, I led him to the house. I could see how impressive it must look, the big garden, the rows of trees, the rhododendrons, hedges and shrubs, no sign of any neighbours. Not the kind of place where you would knock on the door unannounced."

"I had told him that he should come back. He said to me in broken English that he had remembered my saying it. I don't think there was a single word of Dutch in what he said back then. It makes you feel shy too, and so you struggle to find words. We tried to converse using nods and hand gestures. If you'd seen us from a distance, you'd have thought we were both deaf.

"The newspaper had sacked him, because he had overslept once. Which made me want to cancel the newspaper there and then.

"Sometimes I get up early. At six in the morning an entirely different world is stirring and rustling around you. I have to confess that I had often looked out for him, ever since he'd first come to our door. When I had seen an older man getting off his moped by our gate, I had wondered where Ishmaël was, if he was maybe sick, or had been given a different round.

"I asked Ishmaël where he lived. With an Afghan family in town, he said, but he had been asked to leave without any notice. The Afghans had simply deposited his suitcase in the corridor outside. He didn't understand. He hadn't done anything wrong. He'd even looked after the children sometimes, and he paid the rent in advance. And now he had nothing.

"He didn't put it quite like that, of course, but I worked it out. He told me enough for me to understand. On other occasions too, I noticed the way he managed to get his meaning across with his half-swallowed, fragmented sentences, unintentionally challenging me to find my way into his language and to fill in what was missing. He nearly always succeeded in telling me a story I understood.

"The front door was open, and I asked him to please come in. Down the hallway, into my living room, my ordinary enough room which was filled with the collected past. Sixty years of stuff, plus a hundred years of family bits and pieces, paintings, a grandfather clock, photographs from before the war. You'd know all about that, Vince – I remember nearly everything from your room. We could open a little shop together. And call it 'Life's Luggage'.

"Ishmaël didn't sit down. He stood there, dazed, or maybe just numb, that's possible, in the middle of the room. I had no plan whatsoever. I'd more or less mechanically reeled him in and steered him inside. But what now?

"The silence was tangible.

"At one point, I imagined he was so quiet because he liked being with me, that he found it peaceful. Later I realised I'd been wrong. He once confided to me what was going through his head the first time he was in our house. He would have liked to disappear as quickly as possible. What did I want from him? He'd be better off calling a friend he could stay with. He would thank me for my kindness, but he had to go. And then his head was suddenly so muzzy he thought he was going to keel over.

"He asked if he could sit down for a moment, and if I could give him some water, and then he'd leave.

"He looked as if he hadn't eaten for days. I told him to sit while I fetched the water. He was smaller than I remembered, a fragile boy in the corner of my sofa.

"The way I feel with you now: fragile, small, weepy. Sorry.

"Don't look at me like that. It's going to happen now and then, that I run out of words. You don't need to know everything, and don't insist. Oh no, that sounded unkind. I didn't mean it that way. You are the only person who can listen like that and who I can really open up to. You should insist, you know. You're allowed to know everything.

"Yes, I fetched the water. He tentatively took hold of the glass and downed it in one. And said 'Thank you' in that incredible voice, the voice I can't get out of my head. Do you know any way to get rid of things like that, a voice, gestures, a face, eyes?

"No, I don't mean by talking. Talking often seems to me like avoidance, like making noise so you don't have to hear the silence. No, I mean something that would really help. Writing it all down? But then again I don't want to make a drama out of it, even though it might seem that way. How can I move on with a light heart? How can I fit those years with Ishmaël into my life? What's the simplest way to keep hold of the happiness I felt? Isn't it strange that what people call happiness often has a bitter aftertaste? Maybe you understand that, but I don't."

"I asked Ishmaël what his surname was.

"'Bah,' he said. Bah? It took me a second to realise that this was his name. Since that first time, I've simply written his name without any other mental associations, or rather, I used to, because I have no reason to these days. I don't have a clue where he is, and he always chose not to open letters. He didn't like Dutch, although I tried. For years, we sat together, making words and sentences. His reading was coming on, but he wasn't making much progress with his writing. A few capital letters, his own name, a word or two: 'See you tomorrow.'

"I'm getting side-tracked. Where was I? Yes, he was sitting there, and I had walked over to the window and was looking outside, at the bare oaks and the evergreen holly bushes. As if the answer might come from there.

"'You can stay with us for now,' I said to him.

"A sentence from a book. No-one actually says that sort of thing. But I did, on a whim. I hadn't discussed it with Maarten, although it turned out that he was in agreement.

"But Ishmaël shook his head. No, no, he had a friend called Sheppard, he could go to him. That wasn't why he'd come to me. He had lost his job, and I had said that I might be able to help him. All this in fragments of refugee language.

"I had no idea what he could do or what he might want to do, and I certainly couldn't find work for him without notice.

"But I told him I'd find something, that I had to think about it, that I'd discuss it with my husband.

"Discuss it with my husband – what a prim sort of excuse that is. People who say that – I'm going to discuss it with my husband, or with my wife – they're usually looking for some way to put things off and then not do them at all.

"Ishmaël looked at me directly for the first time. Not with disbelief, more like surprise. Or was it simply the face of a man who accepts whatever happens to him, because he's left everything behind?

"Ah, I'm shooting in the dark. How can you know what's behind someone's expression? You can't say anything sensible about a look in eyes you've never seen before. Ishmaël looked at me, yes, and I was glad – there was a sudden moment of connection. But it didn't last long. He turned his head away, seemed startled. Rain hit the window, and somewhere in the house a door slammed.

"'You always bring the rain with you,' I said to him, laughing, but he didn't react. He wasn't much of a one for laughter. He didn't learn how to laugh until much later, and even then he never really got the hang of it.

"I'm jumping about all over the place, I know, but I hope my jumps will take me somewhere. Those very first meetings with him are so long ago now. I feel as if I'm missing something. Somewhere in his first visit to the house there's a clue about how it all ended, about the way he left. What didn't I see?"

"It wasn't the rain or the banging of the door that had startled Ishmaël, but the dog, who had crept in and jumped up next to him on the sofa. I don't believe Africans are that keen on dogs, and newspaper boys certainly aren't. He fended her off before she could lick his face. She's such a sweet dog. You've not met her. Her name's Bijke. Loves everyone, including burglars.

"And that was how it stayed with Ishmaël: every morning, as he came into the garden, she ran up to him, practically trying to hug him, but he held out his arms to keep her away.

"I switched on a couple of lamps and was tempted to light the fire. It was around half past two, usually a sleepy time of day, but not then. I was pretty awake, wide awake in fact. But also uncertain. Ishmaël sat there in silence, frozen, eyes averted, petrified of the dog, who was trying in vain to make friends with him.

"Afterwards – I've often thought about it, always trying to find a reason, something that should have warned me – yes, later I realised that maybe I'd approached him in the wrong way right from the beginning. I should never have made that offer for him to come and stay with us. It was too direct, much too threatening and unexpected, don't you think? That's no way to behave, just springing it on someone like that. It was all too hurried. Well, you know me. I should have sat down quietly with him first, listened to his story as far as possible, and then we could have come up with something together. But I shouldn't have gone rushing in and offered for him to move in with us. We were total strangers. Why would he want to live with us? I say 'us', but he hadn't even met Maarten yet.

"In Africa, there are never any men at home, only women. Men go wandering, or they're dead. A man is often someone who's just passing through. A father is a person of a transient nature – that's one way to put it. I'm generalising, I know. Not all of Africa is the same, but I believe that's how it works in Sierra Leone.

"Sierra Leone, yes, that was where Ishmaël came from. I asked him where he'd lived before, hoping that he would say something, and to wash away the thought of my rash offer.

"He held out his right hand to protect himself and keep the dog in her place. I noticed the pale palm of his hand with its dark edges. It was a moment before he said: 'Sierra Leone.' I tried to remember exactly where it was, that country. I'd never met anyone from Sierra Leone. It was only a place on the map for me, somewhere involving diamonds and a civil war. But that was a long time ago, and it didn't make the headlines anymore. In ordinary everyday life, you never thought about Sierra Leone, never. I know a lot more about it now. I've met people who, like Ishmaël, fled the country, and I know that its terrible civil war never really ended."

"Ishmaël said the name in a whisper, almost apologetically. It sounded as if I really shouldn't attach any importance to it. He wasn't there, he no longer lived there, it was a country of a transient nature. Yes, just like a father. It sounds far-fetched, when I put it like that, but I've thought about it. I'm not just saying it to make some kind of impression. I really feel that if you have no father, then you also have no fatherland. Your map is confused, your compass spins in all directions, you wander and stray.

"A mother always travels with you, no matter where you are. You never lose her. She is there. You *are* your mother and you *have* your father. Or not. To have and to be, two different worlds. Do you know the poem by Ed Hoornik, 'To Have and To Be'? A poet who's been forgotten for years. I would think you could buy his collected works for five euros these days, but he wrote some sublime verse even if he is hardly remembered now. Five euros for a lifelong struggle to compose a few beautiful phrases. A book like that contains a million years of feelings and thoughts, fears and agonies, and endless patience as you try to find the right word.

"Five euros for a life. That's almost like the civil war in Sierra Leone. A life was worth less than that there. Countless deaths, and lives that didn't count.

"Have you ever been to West Africa? I had to look it up to see which countries are there, and which cities. Ivory

Coast, Gambia, Senegal, Liberia, Guinea. Conakry, Bissau, Dakar, Freetown.

"Freetown, such a hopeful name, isn't it? And what a hopeless, filthy and unfree town it was when Ishmaël fled the country and, years later, when he walked up our drive to ask for help. Well, no, it didn't happen quite like that. He didn't exactly ask for help. It was more likely that he had simply returned to an address where someone lived who had spoken to him like a human being. It sounds melodramatic, but that's what it comes down to. I'll probably find myself sounding melodramatic again, but only when I can't find any other way to express myself. Ishmaël was never melodramatic. He didn't know what it was or what it might sound like.

"Like a human being – oh, so you don't think it sounds melodramatic? Good, just as well, but that's beside the point anyway. He was twenty-two years old, or thereabouts. You don't always know the age of a refugee, certainly not the ones without papers. No papers, no passport, no birth certificate, no identity card, the ones who drive the bureaucrats to despair. There's nothing you can do with those people. You can't keep them, and you can't send them away.

"'Totally black and a total blank,' I once heard a civil servant say.

"That's what I meant by 'like a human being'. To a civil servant, you're only a human being when you're documented somewhere as such. And the Netherlands is filled from top to bottom with our fussy fellow citizens. I've seen a lot of them.

Please don't get me started about them. It's become something of a hobbyhorse. They drive you crazy, with their fantasy worlds of data and numbers and files and documents and stamps. You've escaped, you've survived all that terror and misery, your parents have been murdered, you've been uprooted and then you fall into the clutches of one of those bureaucrats or a 'caseworker': and then you'd probably rather be back in Freetown."

"Come on, Vince, let's go down those steps over there, off the dyke. There's a place we can sit a bit further along, with a table and some fairly comfortable benches. There's never anyone else around. I've been there a few times. It's not far from the path to the ferry. Alright?

"I keep getting side-tracked. I'm sorry. It's difficult, so many thoughts that keep coming to me. Talking to you makes me want to talk even more.

"It was the same when I first met you. Twenty-five years ago? I can still picture you coming into our office. Do you remember how, within five minutes, you'd stirred everything up? 'Sensitivity training'. Making little groups and telling one another the truth. Who came up with that idea? Well, yes, it was you, but it was really the management, who'd run out of ideas and were trying a new direction. The director was the first one to take his leave, but otherwise the damage was limited, because you actually did a pretty good job.

"I think you soon turned your back on that sensitivity

business, though. It's odd that we never talked about it again later. Probably because everyone was too embarrassed. Morale and friendship don't respond well to that kind of enforced openness.

"I don't really know what openness is, but people seem to set a great deal of store by it. I'm a bit suspicious of the whole idea of being open, and it's abused a lot too. O.K., in your line of work, it's probably fine. But all those admissions and sighing, all those public revelations; I wonder how honest it really is.

"I'm clearly talking about myself now, too, but I think that's different. I'm not confessing anything. I don't have anything to admit to. If I did, then perhaps my problem might be easier to solve. No, I'm looking for something that could, as it were, close me, not open me up. Something to contain me, something to hold me together. Maybe the opposite of openness.

"What? You don't think so?"

"I asked Ishmaël where he had lived in Sierra Leone, in a city or a village. A pretty pointless question. He grew up in the chaos of war, a time when you don't know where you are and barely where you came from. In any case, he didn't reply.

"I suggested that he should come back the next day. He nodded, as if he'd understood what I'd said, but I wasn't entirely sure he did.

"Bijke jumped off the sofa, rubbed herself against Ishmaël's legs, and Ishmaël very cautiously patted her head, and then she slunk off. Mission failed – that was what Bijke's retreat looked like. She's a wetterhoun, a Frisian water dog, a retriever, a dog that doesn't bite all the way through, but brings back whatever the hunter has shot.

"Ishmaël stood up, and that took courage, as I realise now. Standing up, leaving, putting on a jacket instead of waiting and letting time pass – that was against his nature.

"All the time I knew him, he was always waiting. I believe he thought it was impolite to make the first move. He would wait for someone to shake his hand, for someone to say something to him, for a question to be asked, waiting, waiting. Always ready to go, to keep on running. That too."

"Why don't you ask me something, Vince? You're sitting there so quietly, listening to me, you're like Ishmaël. What time is it? Is it time to stop, shouldn't we go back, you're keeping an eye on the time, aren't you? There'll be a new patient waiting outside your front door at home, while I'm sitting here throwing your practice into confusion.

"Only half an hour? And you really want me to go on?

"It feels as if I've been talking away at you for hours.

"That little body of his. He sometimes worked in the garden with a bare chest, muscular, from a distance so evenly black, without a scratch. As if nothing had happened, as though he'd never run for his life through a thick jungle, pursued, rounded up like an animal. A group of boys, and a few girls, they were fourteen, fifteen years old, so fast and so frightened all through their endless escape. On their way to Freetown, or at least away from their village, where they'd been attacked in broad daylight. It must have been at the beginning of that terrible war. Drugged-up groups of rebels ransacked the land, setting everything on fire, hacking away at everything in sight, abducting women and children.

"In the seven years Ishmaël was with us, he couldn't talk about it. Just one time, but I'm not sure I want to say anything about it, or if I'm even allowed to. By myself, by him, or by the I.N.D., the Immigration and Naturalisation Service.

"The people who work there are relentless, and they have far more influence than anyone else on what this country of ours is going to look like. Politicians are always coming and going, but the I.N.D. just keeps on growing.

"No, that rhymes, but it doesn't quite capture the situation. It's a ghost world, with thousands of doors leading nowhere. You open one, thinking maybe there's a room behind it, but you disappear into a system of corridors that could have been designed by Kafka. That description's not mine – I read it somewhere. But it was my experience too."

"So Ishmaël stood there, looking at the door. He'd probably left his moped by the fence. As I saw him out I pointed to a photograph in the hallway. An old picture of a river, taken by my grandfather on a trip through Africa, I'm not certain where.

"He stopped for a moment and said: 'Moa.'

"'Moa?' I said. He nodded and briefly placed his right hand

on his heart. He did that so many times, for as long as I knew him. Just as a Catholic makes the sign of the cross, unconsciously, without thinking, always that hand on his chest, to the left of centre.

"The Moa's a river in Sierra Leone. But I didn't know that then. Although it might sound odd, that word, Moa, was a sign of trust, of him opening up. I only realised much later that he grew up close to the Moa. That photograph in our hall must have taken him back to his youth, to his father and mother.

"He never mentioned the name again. I guessed its meaning. Moa: homesickness, a flash of memory, of another sun and moon, trees all the way to the water, the cries of birds. Moa, a murmured, sunken word.

"I didn't understand that at the time, though, just stood next to him, on the drive among the puddles, and asked him what he'd said. He didn't reply. I walked with him as far as the gate.

"It took him a moment to take the locks off the moped, stow the chain, put the helmet back on his head. He kept the visor open this time. With his eyes on me, he waved. I don't know what he saw, but his decision must have been made.

"Once he was out of sight, I heard his moped for a while puttering down a nearby lane. Noise carries a long way in our neighbourhood."

"I can barely believe we're sitting here together at the foot of the dyke. After so many years, after all those years together.

But you're hardly asking me anything. Maybe you don't need to. You're a professional, after all, but half an hour's silence does seem like a lot.

"Yes, silence isn't the same as saying nothing. I'm aware of that. I know your philosophy. Now I remember how good you were at that when you came to my office. You led the group with plenty of silences, and that was why the others started to speak up. And it all became rather sensitive."

2

Vincent

Why did I just blurt out that she could come round? In fact, I think I said that she *had* to come.

Tuesday morning, ten o'clock, a week ago, her name on the screen of my telephone. I always kept her number. Whenever I bought a new one, I took the number with me, sometimes thought about deleting it, but never did. I had not ever used it. I didn't even know if she still lived in the same house, or if she had changed her number long ago.

When she appeared at the door, all I could think of to say to her was that it had been almost nine years. Not true, it was yesterday. I feel as if she can see everything just by looking at me. The way I go hot and cold, flush red and then turn pale again. She talks, gesturing with her hands, gently steering me to this picnic spot. I know every movement she makes. Every word sounds as if I'm speaking it myself. I follow her every sigh, her every pause. Ishmaël. I can almost touch him when she tells me about him. She's lost none of her powers of persuasion; I instantly become caught up in her voice and the look on her face.

And now she is sitting here beside me, I remember again

that I was the one who disappeared. For years, I had forgotten what happens in and around me. Nothing has been added; everything has slowly leaked away. I did my work on automatic pilot, talking and listening from hour to hour, from client to client, doing my best to respond intelligently and to give good advice. Fake. Years of camouflage, with psychology as a pretext, and listening to clients so that I would no longer have to do any thinking myself.

I'm going to have to explain to Maria that I have given up my practice. That I only see a few stubborn cases now and then. That no-one's going to be ringing the doorbell.

The people who do come for help are usually their own counsellors. Their appointments with me are first and foremost appointments with themselves, the first few steps towards a different way of life. That is why I kept going. I am hoping they will find something new, go and do something else.

I never managed that myself. I just ended up in a vague fog. I live by touch, doing everything by half measures in a state of semi-consciousness.

The years with Maria went by in a mysterious way, my time with her pulling everything apart. It's strange, the way our love shattered both of our lives. It was like being dragged from reality by some elusive force.

Reality? Do I really imagine that I understand something about life? Nothing exists, everything is in motion, stays out of reach until it disappears. Reality is unreal and unworkable. It's no use to you as a psychologist, or as a human being either.

Maria will see that, with thoughts like that, I soon ran out of clients.

And why I am staring at her now? She wants me to say something. Of course, I have to respond. But I can't tell her just how very much her story touched me, can I? That it almost scares me. She has no idea what she's telling me, she has no way of knowing that I've been underground for nine years now. She found Ishmaël. I found no-one and nothing.

That last evening. As she talks, pointing at the water and some-times seeming to scan the sky above the dyke, I am back there. Elizabeth coming home unexpectedly, Maria and I sitting in the kitchen, at a loss.

I had been anticipating, crawling towards, that moment for months. The years of abandon, dark and light, were over. I could not do it anymore. I felt as if we had pulled our lives to shreds, that nothing would remain if we persisted. Maria was everywhere. I wanted to see nothing and no-one but her. I neglected Elizabeth, the children, my clients, myself.

It was not that I had stopped loving her. It was far worse than that – I could no longer imagine a life without her. And of course I knew she wouldn't give up what she had started long ago: Maarten, her children, her house, her work. Rightly so. That would have made her desperately unhappy. As I became.

"If we ever find out you've got someone else and you want to leave Mam, we never want to see you again."

It is the ultimate threat, something with which no love can

compete. My children said those words to me once, as if they had had some kind of premonition.

The children we never talked about. She didn't bring them up and neither did I. Off limits, too sensitive, far more sensitive even than Maarten and Elizabeth. The ruthless judgment of children, mine and no doubt hers. They would naturally choose the parent who was cheated on and be irreconcilably opposed to the cheat.

And yet, my terrible clumsiness as I told her we had to stop, the stammering, the hash I made of it, is unbearable.

I clutched Elizabeth when she surprised us by appearing in the kitchen, marching right between us. She wasn't supposed to be home until the next day. I couldn't hug her quickly enough.

"You know Maria, don't you? She's been coming for a year." What difference did another lie make, pretending she was a client?

And Maria, she looked at us like a stranger, like someone who had accidentally entered the wrong room. She said goodbye to Elizabeth, to me, and I let her go. She walked into the hallway, through my office, to the door. I watched her opening it, in slow motion. She didn't look back, carefully closing it behind her. That was how it sounded, cautious, so as not to wake anyone, so as not to disturb an idyll. But everything was already disturbed, and that was how it remained.

And now here she is again, sitting beside me.

*

Ishmaël Bah, a name from a stage play. I'm sitting in the stalls, and Ishmaël enters, the only figure on the enormous stage, no prompter, no fellow actors, the lights barely reaching him, he stands as if he is not really there. And he is not, it is an artfully illuminated drawing, just like the real thing. He looks like a person, but he is made up of chalk and light, of Maria's story.

I understand her more than she can suspect. Every detail interests me, all of the events, every attempt she made to find out who Ishmaël was and why he left. It is as if she is talking about me instead of about him. If she thinks she sounds melodramatic now and then, then it's just as well she doesn't know *my* thoughts. I can scarcely stop them, they race on, I struggle to keep up. I am encircled by her – as if I might faint at any moment, that's how it feels.

"We've only been out for half an hour, Maria, I'm asking as few questions as possible, please keep talking, it's going well." Those sentences come from a different part of my brain. It's a form of encouragement I once used all the time: go on, keep talking, my questions aren't that important.

I have to listen to what she's saying. Stay calm, it's Maria sitting there, I have to look at her. Don't think, just watch, and listen to what she wants.

3

Maria

Half an hour? It seems so much longer. Once again, I am lifted up out of time. That was how it always was when we were together. Luckily, he was immediately positive on the telephone when I called him about Ishmaël. Said I should come round, and soon. But now that we're sitting here, I feel that his mind is elsewhere. He looks at me with old eyes, he isn't really listening to my story, his expression isn't right. He's looking for something else.

But it's not about us now. It's about that boy from the Moa River, and I don't know which way to turn. It would be so good if Vincent could show me. But I can see that his thoughts are far away.

His hair is greyer, and it quite suits him. His hands are just as pleasant as ever, as I discovered when he opened the door and held mine for a moment.

I've missed him so very, very much.

"It's been almost nine years," was all he said. Not "How are you?", no hug, no "Take off your coat, come on in" – what do you say in such a situation? "Hey, it's good to see you again"? No, only "It's been almost nine years", as if he'd just been woken from a deep sleep. Had he? No, that's a very different chapter from a very different book.

His face is still the same, not really handsome, but attractive. He'll probably be giving up his practice soon. He's sixty-four now. Four years younger than me – I was glad about that at the time. I always found it hard to believe that we only really got to know each other when I was in my mid-fifties.

Five years so close, it's incredible that no-one noticed anything. We decided to break up just before my sixtieth, and a year later Ishmaël arrived. He seemed very young and very old at the same time, a frail body with sad eyes.

Maybe it's a bit crazy, but he sometimes reminded me of Vince. No, I'm not going to tell him everything that's going through my mind now, definitely not. It's just as well he can't hear my thoughts. He'd only start mulling it all over and bringing things up again, and then we'd be talking about him and me.

"Almost nine years"? Eight years, eleven months and nineteen days, you mean. Did he think I didn't know, did he think a single day has gone by without my being reminded of him, reminded of us?

In the beginning, I wanted to go to him at every moment of the day and night. I wanted to hear his voice, kept stopping myself just before calling him. I walked endlessly along the river in his direction. It was too far to walk, of course, I knew that, but it made me feel as if nothing had happened, that I was just going to see him as usual. Hours on the dyke, with Bijke, through the cows to the water, along a breakwater, counting the boats slowly coming by. That was how I distracted myself for a whole year.

No, I have to focus on Ishmaël, on that constant, vague sadness that he left behind. I'm walking on loose sand, I'm sixty-eight and there are still so many places I want to see, but I don't know which way to go. I can't sit vacantly at home, spinning on my own axis, can I?

Maybe going to see Vince wasn't such a good idea, but I had called him before I had thought it through. He was always one telephone number away from me. I know it by heart. How many thousands of messages must we have sent each other? All told, it must have been a book's worth. I called him almost automatically. I couldn't imagine anyone else – he's the only one I want to talk to.

Who we were together, the way our nomadic existence played out, I've managed to process it in those nine years, accepted it – what else could I do? I wasn't even afraid to see him anymore.

Cut it out. I have to stop this now, it makes no sense. This is how you end up sailing into a troubled dream. I'm here for Ishmaël, for that lost boy. He is draining me, and I so want to be rid of it, of him, of that rootless feeling.

4

Vincent

"Don't think." That's what I said to her all those years ago. And to myself. And indeed, we didn't do much thinking after that. Stockholm, Grand Hotel, winter 2001. They were staying there, and I had a conference, which I'd signed up for at the last minute, and then I heard that she was going to be there with her family. It never stopped snowing and the hotel bar was packed. Tour boats drew up to the quayside and sailed slowly back out into the snowflakes that danced above the water. Blurred silhouettes of buildings, a bridge, a group of trees, silent cars, a horse sleigh with tourists, seagulls on a moored boat. Through the enormous windows of the hotel, you looked out onto a world from a children's book.

"Anton Pieck," she said, pointing outside. She pointed with my hand, holding it naturally, as if we had always been together. I had grabbed hers just before, as if by accident. It was a deliberate accident, though, I couldn't wait any longer, I was drawn towards her, and could think of one thing only, of touching, being touched, taking her hand in mine. I thought it was an act of great courage. Maarten and her son were out on a tour boat in the harbour and would be gone for some time. Out of everything that happened then and afterwards, that was the most glorious moment: her hand in mine, our hands pointing at a scene from a fairy tale.

Don't think. Feel – the motto of that day, the motto of all our years. High-level deception.

A little later, she was standing again at the wide window in the bar, with Maarten beside her and their son, who had both returned happy from their trip. The snow had stopped. She waved calmly at me when I walked past outside, as if a small landslide had not just occurred.

Always those two scenes from Stockholm. They slip into my mind, and I am unable to stop them. I've given up trying, they appear whenever they please. Now, for instance, they're intruding again. Stockholm, Grand Hotel, the snow and the boats and us.

I have to listen. Yes, I can hear her, and I'll help her if I can.

Ishmaël, he must have felt forever lost. Child of war, child of murdered parents, child of an escape and an endless journey to a foreign land full of incomprehensible people. A lost boy. An abandoned boy.

She circles around his secret. She is a falcon spotting a mouse. But is there really a secret? I try to put myself in their positions, in Maria's, in his. It's not easy.

The years with her may have hollowed him out, impercept-ibly. I can imagine that her love and attention and dedication, little by little, turned his life inside out. A life that had already been churned up.

It wouldn't surprise me if she tells me he had suicidal thoughts. He must have done. Driven out of a village in the jungle, only to end up in a world of limitless wealth and pressure. He has been uprooted. He distrusts himself and everyone else, he lives in a body he no longer feels to be his own. Is it something like that? Maybe, maybe not. I realise that I am resorting to made-up explanations. Uprooting, fear, futility, hopelessness, depression – they're words, labels, attempts to understand something that cannot be understood. All old psychology. That profession of mine weighed more heavily on me as the years went by. I feel that the textbooks should be rewritten, that there were problems and worlds we did not know. That was, indeed, already the case when Maria and I were still together. I became stuck.

Under Ishmaël's skin, something is happening that we cannot fathom. At least I can't. His disappearance is mysterious, something almost sacred. It's a foolish thought, of course. Sacred – what's that word doing here? What does it even mean?

It's just as well Maria can't hear me. She wouldn't believe her ears. More than that, she wouldn't recognise me. But I'm still the same person. Still the man whose hand she lifted up in one overwhelming moment.

If only we were back in that snowy landscape. Or in De Rijp. I wonder if she remembers that. Black ice, between banks of shovelled snow. She led the way, skating faster than me. I followed in the trail of her broad strokes. Sometimes she let me catch up, we skated next to each other, glove in glove.

I have retraced that journey in my mind hundreds of times: the moon suddenly appearing above the horizon, not far from the village, on the last stretch, with no-one ahead of us. It couldn't be called skating – it was a dream. I see again the snow slowly beginning to fall, half of the sky dark grey and the other half still blue. A world split in two, with us moving through it, towards the café, into the dusk, the last hour together before heading for our homes.

We consisted of eyes and hands and few words. Around us, the voices of cheerful skaters in the café, everyone talking to everyone else, someone playing a piano, you could hardly open the door for all the rucksacks and jackets and skates piled up behind it. An explosion of happiness on a few square metres of wooden floor.

Did Ishmaël just stop coming? Did he disappear overnight? Were there no clues, was she absolutely unprepared?

It was too much for him. He didn't know what to do with her love, he couldn't cope with all that help, all that well-meaning friendship, which could not be repaid. It piled up, month after month, year after year. Encircling him. He had to be a foster child, and he would become a son. No, I'm afraid that won't work. I understand her feeling of abandonment so well, but his eventually leaving was inevitable. He was not what she had thought or hoped – he was a refugee, passing through. For a few years, he had found shelter.

Sinterklaas and Christmas and birthdays and holidays, she had had them all with him, and it made her feel that he had come home. But that is not home. He doesn't know home the way we do. Home is a threat – and that is where it all went wrong. Home is another word for murder, for your mother being dragged away.

She wanted to absorb him into her existence, into her way of life, but that seems impossible to me.

I'm rambling. I'm not going to tell her anything of these thoughts I'm having. I'm not even sure any of it is true. You say something and at that moment it changes. The experiences of a boy from Africa – what would I know about that? Presumably it's all very different from what we can surmise with all our psychology. Maybe our laws don't apply to him at all, maybe other forces are at play here.

She asked if we should go back to my practice. I need to tell her that I don't have a practice now. Funny, she talked about a new patient who might ring the doorbell. Patient? I hope she was using the word ironically. That sounds more like a hospital. But it's me, Maria. It's Vince.

She looks at me as if she is looking *for* me. I'm not a psychologist anymore, Maria. I'm your lover. Nothing's changed. I forgot my profession the moment I saw you again.

5

Maria

"Look at us sitting here in silence, Vince. I'm sorry. I shouldn't have called you. I think it's better if I go home. I can see you're not enjoying this. Your mind's elsewhere, and I can understand that. It was foolish of me to ambush you like this. I'm starting to get side-tracked too. But it shouldn't be about us today.

"Really? Do you mean that? You honestly think it's good that we're talking about Ishmaël? Do you believe it'll help? That was my thinking when I came to you, of course.

"But you have to promise me that you'll tell me when you've had enough. I'm not one of your patients, although it seems I am when I hear myself talking like this. You have to tell me right away, Vince."

"I feel as if my life stopped abruptly on the day Ishmaël stopped walking up the drive. He was there every day. I often didn't even hear him coming in, but when I opened the kitchen door in the morning, there he was, with Bijke beside him.

"It might sound silly, but if you asked me what he did all day, I couldn't tell you exactly. Odd jobs. He spent a lot of time in the shed, mowed the grass, chopped wood for the fire. He had a spot at the bottom of the garden where he often slept. He was simply *there*.

"At first, he used my surname and called me 'Mevrouw'. It's a word that always troubled me a little, 'Mevrouw'. It's like a thin roller blind that someone lets down. I've never got used to it. When someone says 'Mevrouw', they immediately take a step backwards, inaudibly, imperceptibly.

"Ishmaël didn't know that, or maybe he did, but anyway, at some point, he stopped saying it. And he called me Maria.

"He spoke my name carefully, as if hesitating every time. Was it allowed? Did he dare? But I'd asked him so many times to call me by my first name that he couldn't avoid it any longer.

"The first time was after six months. It was in the summer, I was sitting in the garden when I heard him, soft but urgent.

"'Maria?'

"And again: 'Maria?', because I didn't look up at first, even though I'd heard him. I couldn't believe my ears. 'Maria', he'd said it, and there was no way back. We were still entangled in those kinds of little skirmishes in the early days. Now it seems childish, but back then it mattered.

"He'd had to return his moped to the newspaper delivery company, so he walked from the small flat where he lived to our house, an hour there, an hour back. He didn't think that was out of the ordinary, he didn't want things to be any different. He had a bike, but he rarely used it.

"I hoped he'd be able to get his driving licence and become a courier or something like that, I still had expectations. I know all the traffic rules now, Vince. We sat there next to each other, for two years, drumming them into ourselves. They ask some bizarre questions, those people at the driving test centre. It's a sort of immigration service for traffic.

"'There's a tram coming from the right, and an ambulance coming from a residential area on the right with flashing lights, but no siren. Who has priority?' A trivial little question, and soon a piece of cake.

"Ishmaël passed, pretty unusual for a semi-literate man, you might think, but guessing is a skill that can be learned. And then the practical, failed twice, got it third time. Looking back, it's hard to understand, but still, they opened the door for him a crack, he could go into the world, they let him through, across the threshold. Only he didn't go. It was the same with everything."

"Why had he called me on that day? You're right, you've sensed that I have left something out. Something I've wanted to think about as little as possible since then.

"A letter had come from Sierra Leone, in English, and he couldn't read it, at least that's what he said. He was probably just lucky with that driving theory test. He must have done a lot of guessing with the multiple-choice questions, even if he could more or less understand what was on the paper by then. He could also decipher the sports pages of the newspaper by the end. I'm not sure if he wasn't faking it a little with his illiteracy, if he didn't know more he let on. I sometimes wondered if he didn't at some point go to school after all.

"But anyway. That letter. He gave it to me, his name was on it, Mr I. Bah, with four different addresses scribbled criss-cross on the envelope. It had been forwarded from the Sierra Leone embassy in Belgium, to the asylum seekers' centre in Den Bosch, to the asylum seekers' centre in Alphen aan de Rijn, and even to the address in Colmschate where he had stayed for a couple of months. You could read a life just by looking at the envelope. Sender: Sierra Leone Tribunal, Free-town. I was shocked. The letter had been travelling for some time, from one place to another. And how long had Ishmaël had it?

"I didn't ask. He simply handed it to me, turned around and pretended he had something to do in the shed. He hadn't opened the envelope. It was a letter meant to be passed on. I had the urge to pop it back into a letterbox, to some other I. Bah – apparently everyone's called Bah in Sierra Leone.

"The sun was shining, Bijke was padding around after Ishmaël, and I sat down on the grass, half nervous, half curious. The Sierra Leone Tribunal, it must be to do with Taylor, and that hideous civil war and its unending murder and torture. I only knew the broad outlines of the story. What do we know about what goes on in Africa, after all? But, along with Ishmaël, Africa had entered my home, and by the time I held that letter in my hands, I had already discovered more about the total anarchy and the horrors in Sierra Leone. Not from Ishmaël, though. He never said anything about his homeland.

"They were looking for him, Vince. He was being summoned before the tribunal in Freetown. They wanted to interview him as a witness against a man called Johnny Kumala. The name meant nothing to me. The bottom line was that Ishmaël might have seen a certain village being attacked and the villagers massacred, the village of I. Bah, who had fled to the Netherlands.

"The name of the village was the name I once saw in his file. I can't even pronounce it, it's basically just a bunch of consonants, and I don't want to say it either, because everything in that file is unspeakable and secret. Ishmaël allowed me to read the file just once. He wanted me to keep it for him.

"No, I'm not going to tell you anything about it, because it's *his* story. It's at home in the safe, a few pages, typed by someone from the I.N.D., signed by Ishmaël. Well, it looks more like an inkblot than a signature. How ridiculous to ask someone who most likely can't read or write to sign his statement. A typically Dutch request."

"Johnny Kumala turned out to be one of the murderous sidekicks of Charles Taylor, the man behind all the crimes that were committed in Sierra Leone. You have no idea how bad it was, you can't understand how the country can still exist, how there are any people left.

"I tore the summons in two. I walked down the garden, fetched a shovel, and buried it in a deep hole, as if it were a dead pet. The funeral of a letter.

"Ishmaël never asked me what was in that letter, and I never said anything to him about it. We acted as if nothing had happened. Gone and forgotten.

"You may not agree with what I did. Some things can't be buried, you're right about that, but at that moment it was the best I could come up with.

"I wasn't myself, I was panicking, I had to get rid of that letter as quickly as possible. That letter was Ishmaël's old life, I wanted to keep it away from him. I didn't want him to be confronted with this summons from a world he had been so lucky to escape.

"How long does paper take to decompose? A year, five? The tribunal's long over now. Out of that entire organised mas-sacre, which went on for ten years, I believe they arrested and sentenced fifteen men. Most of them are dead now. Taylor's serving a life sentence in a cell in England.

"And Kumala was acquitted."

"The sun was shining, yes, I can still remember how terribly hot and muggy it was the day we heard about the acquittal. It must have been normal for Ishmaël, an African day, but for us it was out of the ordinary.

"I gained an extra shadow, that was how it felt. As if it was constantly attached to me. A sort of doppelganger that follows you around and you can't it shake off. Maybe the correct term is a bad conscience.

"Johnny Kumala was acquitted because of a lack of evidence. Did I bury that evidence in the ground? Did I have it in my hands and do nothing with it?"

6

Vincent

"No, Maria. There's absolutely no point thinking like that and taking a burden of guilt upon your shoulders. There's no guilt here, not for you, and not for Ishmaël. Those criminals are the guilty ones, and it seems only a handful of them were caught.

"I just wanted to say that we have plenty of time. There's no-one waiting at my door, so we can sit here for a while. Did you notice that the ferry has been back and forth at least a dozen times? The ramp on the quay, the rattling of the chain – the sounds of long ago."

She buried Ishmaël's letter in the ground.

Where did all our letters go? I sent them to her at work, most often from Utrecht. I was lecturing there two days a week. She sent hers to my hotel, and there was sometimes a little stack of them waiting for me at the reception.

The Janskerkhof in the rain, on a Tuesday evening, the braying of boys who have had too much beer – you have to be pretty robust if you don't want it to spoil the mood. But it wasn't a problem for me, because she was there. Love goes to your legs and feet, making you light, so it's ten times easier to walk. It's a shame the same doesn't apply to thinking. I suspect those lectures of mine made little impression, perhaps all they noticed was my muddled and clumsy teaching. Poor students.

I used to stay at the Malie Hotel. I remember cutting the address off the writing paper in the room. It was automatic, to hide my tracks. I signed with a V.

"My dearest V," she wrote back.

In the beginning, our love was mainly on paper. She called me Cyrano. Writing made the smallest of things epic.

We wrote to each other before we touched one another. After Stockholm, it still took a few more months. By the time I first saw her naked, I'd already undressed her in so many letters. But she was so much more beautiful in real life. The glow of her, the gleam of her eyes. Her arms around me, her hand on the back of my head, the lightness of her body.

Don't think.

How she managed to make those occasional visits to Utrecht is a mystery to me now. Back then, it only delighted me. I probably did not even ask her about it, she was there, and that was enough. She knew the city, she had studied there, she took me to bars where poets drank, and musicians. I knew nothing about those people, hadn't ever read their books or listened to their music. She had. She was way ahead of me.

The side room downstairs in the former Hotel des Pays Bas was packed. Half past five in the afternoon, and they were

47

already taking down the stalls of the flower market outside. Maria took me with her to a reunion of her music school. She had a couple of hours before the last train. She only just made it.

By then, I knew how well she had once played and how sorry everyone was that she'd stopped. But I had no idea who all those people were who were hugging Maria like the prodigal daughter. She was radiant, I saw her surrounded on all sides, how loved she was, how much they had missed her.

A small Gypsy band was playing. Definitely not conservatory music, which was probably why it had been chosen. So that no-one would feel offended. I heard Maria saying hello to people, Janine, Emmy, Zino, names that meant nothing to me. At the time. That evening Maria was absorbed into a different, lighter world, a world that was wonderful and new to me, a world to which she had said farewell, but which had without warning caught up with her for a moment.

The melancholy musicians played on, the glasses never becoming even half empty, and I could not take my eyes off her. Of course, I asked her when she was going to start playing again. She shook her head, smiling but firm. She had found a new instrument, she said, and she gave my arm a quick stroke and laughed.

It was our first year. Outside, it was summer.

It was only after we had stopped seeing each other that I began reading poems, going to concerts and bookshops. It was as if

I were chasing after her, as if subconsciously hoping to bump into her somewhere. Which never happened. Yet it gave me a kind of peace, to know that she had been there, that she had walked in those places. Senseless attempts to be close to her. My quest doomed to failure, my emotions gone haywire.

After that evening in our kitchen, I never held Elizabeth again, not once. I avoided every approach she made. Pathetic of me.

I feel that I'm beginning to understand Ishmaël a little. It's odd, I don't know him, I don't know how it could be possible. Not wanting to come home, not wanting to run the risk of having to leave again. Is that what was behind his disappearance?

But is he really gone? How does Maria know that for sure? Maybe he's still around. Maybe he hasn't left the Netherlands at all. It makes me want to track him down for her.

"I'm sorry, Maria, that I'm not saying much, but I can hear you loud and clear. It's a strange link to make, but watching that ferry going back and forth, I suddenly remembered the first time I went to Florence, a week at a conference. I don't think I've told you about this before, but stop me if I have.

"I skipped most of the sessions, preferred to go into the centre of the city instead. I started talking with a North African who was selling what looked like luxury handbags and sunglasses, but everything was fake. No big deal, the boy was nice, and I stayed there with him, sitting on a folding chair in the middle of the street, close to piazza della Repubblica, with what must have been ten other Africans, who also had their wares on display. All afternoon.

"He spoke a mixture of English and Italian, but I could understand him just fine. He told me how he'd ended up in Italy. There was no mass migration at the time, he'd simply come over on a boat, illegally though, of course. But the people in Florence tolerated him, and the police rarely interfered.

"He lived everywhere and nowhere, and that was how he liked it, he didn't want anything else. That whole afternoon he sold one single bag, the cheapest, and it was haggled down by half too. Mo, that's what they called him.

"He lived like a refugee, but he wasn't one. He was happy, he was free of his country and his family, he didn't have to answer to anyone, he sat there on his chair for as long as he wanted, drank coffee, watched the sky and the girls, and he was contented, he said.

"A nice story, but I'm under no illusion that what Mo told me was true. It was just as fake as his bags, 'made in Italy'. He wished it was true, that one day it would *become* true. But why didn't I forget it? Why am I telling you about it now? Maybe there was some kind of hidden truth in it after all.

"Mo, I can still see him: a handsome face, sunglasses high up among his curls, and a T-shirt with the Leaning Tower of Pisa on it. He'd just come from there, he told me. He wanted another T-shirt like it, but with the Ponte Vecchio instead."

7

Maria

"No, you hadn't told me that story, Vince. So the boy's at home wherever he can put down his chair and sell his bags. Is that what you mean? That's kind of you, it's almost as if you kept the story for me all this time."

Shall I tell him I went to Freetown not long ago? And to the Moa River, and that I found Ishmaël's village, with its unpronounceable name? I'm not sure. No-one knows. Not even Maarten. He would have stopped me, he'd have kept nagging at me about it until I gave up on the plan.

Is Vince waiting for me to say something? The way he's sitting – it's so familiar. Legs crossed, one hand on the back of his neck, head at a slight angle, eyes on the water. But he's looking increasingly uncomfortable.

At first, I wanted to get away as soon as I could, but not now. I want to stay, it's quiet here, soothing. I've not felt embraced like this in ages. As if he's holding me tight. Just sitting beside him gives me peace.

If he knew how unhappy I was on that trip to the Moa River.

He clearly suspects that Ishmaël is an obsession for me. But no, I don't believe it is. That would make it a sickness. I didn't come to him because I'm ill, but because I don't want to become ill.

My mind is still pretty good, and even though it hurts all over when I get up in the morning, that passes fairly quickly. And I could have the whole day ahead of me to do things. But I can't get started on anything without worrying. Since Ishmaël left, I'm disoriented, I don't have any direction. I look back, and the further I look, the more barren and empty my life seems.

I would like to talk to him about why that is, I had hoped he might be able to make some sense of it. He knew me before I lost my equilibrium, he knew me better than anyone.

A friend of mine once called Ishmaël my noble savage. Apparently that was the way I talked about him. But that's nonsense, Ishmaël wasn't a noble savage, whatever that might once have meant, far from it, even though he grew up without any schooling in the forest beside a river. I was annoyed that she put it that way, and it also frustrated me that I had no proper way to describe Ishmaël. I still don't. He's been gone a year now, and I simply cannot explain who he really was. But whenever I attempt to characterise him, I just end up saying something about myself.

What point is there in describing someone? The colour of his eyes, his voice, he walks a bit like so-and-so, he's quick-tempered, funny, always reacts like this or that, you name it, good or bad, and still you know nothing. Descriptions are a dead end. All that counts is the absence. He's not there anymore, something's been taken away from inside me. What remains is a feeling of loss, stifling me and hemming me in.

Yes, I'm about to say something, don't worry, Vince, don't look away.

His shirt looks new. Matches his jacket. He hasn't changed one bit.

8

Maria

"I visited his village, Vince, I haven't been back from Sierra Leone that long. For three weeks, I was in Ishmaël's homeland instead of where I said I was. I'd told Maarten I really wanted to make a trip to France on my own. That was fine by him, he was busy with his own life.

"Three weeks – it seems like an ocean of time. But it trickled away into the landscape, into the river, into the villages, into the endless number of people. I've been back two months now, but sometimes I wonder if I was ever there at all.

"My first time in Africa. I don't think you've been there, have you? I remember you saying you're a European through and through. You thought Rome was far enough, you didn't need to go any further than that, did you? And maybe you're right. A white person in Africa, it's not right. I was suddenly very aware of my colour."

"An utterly insane venture, that's what it was. Maarten has no idea I was there, he doesn't need to know, he wouldn't understand.

"And it seems you don't either.

"But, then again, it wasn't that impulsive. I was convinced that going to where he was born would make it easier for me to understand why he had run away from us. I kept wondering if the contrast between our world and his was so huge that the two can never truly be reconciled. And if that was perhaps why he had disappeared. But I also wanted to see if that gulf really was as wide as I had supposed. And, if I'm being honest, I obviously hoped to hear some news of Ishmaël, too. But Sierra Leone brought me down to earth with a bang, and it was very hot earth too. The heat there really gets to your head.

"The journey from Freetown to the Moa River took an eternity. Roads in that part of the world are just one pothole after another. There are no trains – a Jeep is the only thing that will handle the journey.

"Every bend in the road was followed by another. We meandered across the country, losing all sense of direction. One minute you're looking at mountains, the next you're in the middle of dense forest with the cries of animals all around.

"And meanwhile I had plenty of time to think about what I'd seen the night before."

"I'd arrived at my hotel, in the centre of Freetown. It's one of the few places where Westerners stay. An old, worn-out building, without any glamour.

"In the middle of the lobby stood a man who looked like a boxer, ready for a fight. He had an entourage of sunglasses around him. And his were the biggest sunglasses of all. Whatever they were planning to do was clearly something that could not stand the light of day.

"I asked the porter who they were. He said something about 'friends of the president'. I suddenly imagined it was what Johnny Kumala looked like, but he had disappeared. He wouldn't dare show his face in public these days.

"An agitated buzz went around the room. One of the men from the gang sauntered over to a waiting photographer. Apparently he'd taken a picture. He was told to hand over his camera, but he protested. A second man broke away from the gang of sunglasses, and the photographer fell silent.

"I was watching, the porter whispered something, but I didn't understand him. No-one did anything, everyone was silent, I could hear music from the speakers, which I hadn't noticed before.

"Then another group of sunglasses stepped out of the lift and into the lobby. I immediately recognised the man in the middle. It was Tony Blair. What was *he* doing there?

"The first group made a brief attempt to speak to the second group. There was a commotion, they were turned away. Blair looked neither left nor right, his men shielded him expertly. The boxers slunk off. The photographer stood there watching with empty hands, resigned to it. End of press moment, end of camera. Someone called out a name. No, it didn't sound like Kumala. The conversations in the hotel resumed, telephones rang, the tension ebbed away.

"A sinister guy tries to talk to a world leader. A man with a trail of victims, that was what he looked like. The kind of man who had attacked Ishmaël's village, for instance.

"He had some nerve to attempt to infiltrate Blair's circle. Criminal and accomplice. Blair, one of the elusive architects of total chaos.

"So what was he doing in Freetown? He was probably there to do business in diamond land. Brits in search of old alliances in their former colony. And the boxer-in-charge, whatever his name was, had perhaps been able to evade the Tribunal – because of a lack of evidence, a lack of witnesses?"

"There were four of us: the driver, two men and me. The other three were constantly talking, or rather yelling, to make themselves heard above the noise of the engine. Their language is incomprehensible, with not a single word to hold onto. Yes, phone, I made out that word, it's used all over the world, I think. It's just like here, they live inside their mobiles, they worship the things, it's an obsession.

"My driver was a man from the region where I wanted to go. I'd asked at a tourist office if they knew of anyone like that. There are in fact tourists out there again, heading off on adventurous treks through the Moa region, wildlife types with zip-off trousers and hats. I'd made a note of the name of the village that was mentioned in that letter from the Tribunal and in Ishmaël's file.

57

"We arrived in the pouring rain, in a totally apathetic village. I learned nothing there.

"No-one seemed interested in Ishmaël Bah. Yes, a few families called Bah had lived there, but they'd all fled, or been murdered by Taylor's rebels. Wasn't there anyone left, not a single Bah?

"I had pictures of Ishmaël with me, taken in our garden, a whole series of them. Maybe they knew his family? I obviously didn't say I was looking for him. The people I spoke to shook their heads. But one woman held the photographs for longer, looked at them one by one, and then again. I noticed her hand was shaking, as if she'd been struck by a sudden fever. She dropped a couple of prints, quickly picked them up again, clumsily brushed the mud off. Finally she returned them to me.

"No, yes, could be, the face reminded her of someone, but it was a long time ago.

"I walked to the river, not far from the village. Ishmaël must have been there often as a child. The Moa is fast-flowing. Some of the trees are up to their waists in water. There's a sort of anger emanating from the river, from the whirling waves. Little waterfalls everywhere, birds skimming over them, a dazzling kingfisher. I sat for hours on a tree trunk, just watching.

"But I didn't find Ishmaël anywhere, not the merest glimpse of him. I couldn't picture him living there, in the forests around me, by the steaming river, in the lethargic village. Nothing reminded me of him."

*

"You're obviously wondering what on earth I hoped to find there. His father and mother, other family members? People who would welcome me and want to help me? Perhaps so.

"In the Jeep on the way there, I imagined finding his mother. Just like that. A romantic thought, a sentimental idea, but still I had a kind of hope.

"It was magical thinking. That I'd show her the photographs and she'd throw her arms around me. All the ideas you get in your head on such a journey. So I was set up for disappointment. The village could never live up to my fantasies.

"Perhaps the people there weren't lethargic at all, maybe they really were curious and interested. They were modest, didn't want to make any hasty statements, they probably saw that I'd embarked on a hopeless quest. So many people were missing. Dead family members are more the rule than the exception.

"That I was there, walking around the village with photographs of Ishmaël Bah, was like the world turned upside down. They should be the ones with photographs, but everything was gone, the history, the family, the houses, nothing remained, everything washed away in the violence. Asking about it was offensive. You don't do that kind of thing: it's summoning death."

"But that one woman – I keep thinking about her. She was the only one who really knew something. Even though she pretended Ishmaël was a just some young boy, like so many others that have come and gone, that woman must have recognised him. She was the one who walked with me to the Jeep when I left her village behind and headed back to civilisation. She waved. I think it was meant for Ishmaël.

"Was she his mother? It's possible, isn't it? That she made a swift decision not to recognise him, because otherwise this woman standing there would have to bring her son back. Ishmaël would be torn away from the safety of Europe, back into the obscurity of a village on the banks of the Moa, having no prospects. A split second to make that decision. To act as if the boy in the photograph seemed vaguely familiar, yes, that face, could be. No, maybe not, oh, so many boys went missing back then.

"Ishmaël, her son, escaped all the misery and was in good hands. Don't let on, don't show any emotion.

"Would a mother be able to do such a thing? What do you think? The intensity of her waving as I left – why else would she have waved that way?

"At the edge of the village, where we'd left the Jeep, I stopped for a moment to talk to her, or rather, my driver made an attempt to translate what she said. Nothing special, just that she wished me a safe journey home, something like that. And then she shook my hand.

"It's possible, isn't it, Vince? It could have been her.

"But even if it was, Ishmaël isn't here anymore. I can't tell him about it, and would he be pleased to hear the news anyway?

"As we turned the Jeep to go back to Freetown, the woman walked beside the vehicle for some way. The last thing I saw was her arm raised in the air."

9

Vincent

I really don't know what to make of her trip to this Moa River. Not only was it dangerous, it seems more than anything like a futile attempt to get Ishmaël back.

What if that woman really was his mother? And what if she had said, "It's him! Where is he?" Maria would not have been able to answer that question and then the misery would have been compounded. Her son had been found, and yet he hadn't. She would have done that mother a terrible injustice by just turning up with a photograph and nothing else. The mother would have lost him twice.

What was she doing there, and what did she expect to achieve, except for disappointment and pain? Was she trying to heal the world? To bring a son back to his mother? To let them know that Ishmaël was alive, in the Netherlands, or wherever he is, in Germany or Belgium or Sweden? He's alive, I took care of him, we were together for a few years, but he moved on. Something like that?

It's possible that it was his mother, that woman. Almost unbelievable, but possible. That she realised that she must not recognise her son, in order to protect him from herself, from her village and her homeland. No greater love.

Freetown, a name worth repeating. Freetown. You hear music, it's a place where people dance. I can't imagine Maria in that city. She thinks I've never been to Africa, but that's not the case. I never wanted to tell her that I went there with Irene just after graduation and travelled from north to south. And again it strikes me how much Irene and Maria are alike. The same tone, the same temperament, the same movements, at times the same ironic look.

She's long gone, dead before I got to know Maria. And our relationship didn't even survive that trip. But Africa is Irene, Africa is an accumulation of memories, it's where I became an adult. An adult? Well, less naive and less innocent, in any case.

We were twenty-five. We lived on and over and inside each other. Maria would probably see it as a betrayal, the fact that I never spoke to her about it. Betrayal of Irene, I mean. But I don't think it would be kind to talk to Maria about an old love, about someone who was so like her. She's dead, and yet that doesn't matter. In my past, she is alive and we are travelling together. Egypt, Sudan, Ethiopia, Somalia, Kenya, Tanzania, South Africa. I know the map by heart, the route, the cities, Cairo, Khartoum, Addis Ababa, Mogadishu, Nairobi, Dar es Salaam, Lourenço Marques, Cape Town.

We meandered along, driving the third-hand Jeep we had bought in Cairo and would sell to a dealer who bought old iron in Cape Town. At last we made it, only to leave everything behind, first and foremost our love, which we had thought would last forever. We drove ourselves into a corner. We returned home empty and sad.

Irene. She refuses to disappear, always popping back up again when I'm not paying attention. It's not unpleasant, I don't resent her for it, but sometimes it's hard.

It's because of Freetown, because of Ishmaël, because of a chain of associations. Irene has joined them, uninvited and, right now, not altogether welcome.

Just before she died, in a hospital on the A1, I went to see her. She was too hot. She'd pulled off the blankets, her night-dress had ridden up, she was wearing pale-blue underpants. All I really wanted to do was lie down beside her, alone with her one last time. The heat was rolling off her, and she looked wild.

I said: "Do you remember Dar es Salaam?"

"When are we going?" she said. She seemed delirious. A doctor came in and asked me to say goodbye, as a longer visit would be too tiring for the patient.

I can still hear him saying it. Too tiring – she had less than a day to live.

Irene took my hand, told the doctor I could stay and that he should leave. I sat there like that for a while, and before long I heard her mumble: "Keep on the left, Vince, they drive on the left here."

Those were her last words. To me at any rate.

*

Freetown, I wish I could have gone there with Maria. We never had time, but in my mind I went all over the world with her. We only travelled in bed, where we stepped out of time. It was the illusion of a journey, a new one every time. There wasn't much more we could do, both tied down, beholden to families, work, friends and appointments. There were only those endless hours when we thought about each other, but couldn't see each other.

10

Maria

Was it a mistake to come and see him? He's listening, but he doesn't seem to be hearing anything. He's so quiet, staring across the water. He's looking at a time that's over and gone.

I am over and done with it. What he sees no longer exists. What is under my clothes has slowly but surely died. I mean my heart, not what he might be thinking about. That's still functioning, my body doesn't look bad. He thought I was beautiful, sometimes I did too, not always but sometimes, especially when he looked at me. He undressed me in the riskiest of places, where we might be discovered at any moment.

The chance that a secret might be discovered is half the excitement, he said one time. Every relationship that needs to be camouflaged is driven by the fear and the hope of coming out into the open, visible to everyone, naked and exposed. No way back, and no way forward, discovered and forever buried.

It went on for five years, and no-one knows about it, there's not even any secret now, as there's no chance of being found out. We talk like adults, we sit side by side in a conspiracy of questions and answers: psychologist meets woman in distress, lets her tell her story, rarely asks anything, just listens and looks.

And through everything the past slips silently into our conversation. I am like the woman I once was, when I met him for the second time. Fourteen years ago.

11

Maria

"Dear Vince, do you mind if I head home now? The wind's getting up, and I'm a bit chilly. I came on the bus and the stop's not far – would you walk me there? I rather dropped all this on you, didn't I? You must be pretty tired of me."

"No, no, not at all, Maria. Not at all. Yes, I'll walk you to the bus, of course I will. Why don't we meet up again on Friday? You've told me such a lot, and I need some time to let it sink in. Your incredible trip to Sierra Leone, that woman, Freetown.

"Are you free then? Shall we talk at my place? It's less windy there. And Elizabeth isn't home during the day."

"I can come any time, Vince. Great, I'll see you on Friday."

Elizabeth isn't there during the day, he said. He mentioned her name without any hesitation, and it sounded neutral. So he's still with her. Just as well. A divorce was precisely what he was trying to avoid.

I never really wanted to find out anything more about her. It has nothing to do with any feelings of guilt, which is strange, it should have, but I've always seen our relationship as something guiltless.

Elizabeth. I thought she was beautiful, like the sound of her name. The few times I saw her, she was entirely herself, independent. I could see why Vince married her. There was something masculine about her. Short black hair, soft-grey eyes.

But generally she stayed in the shadows. Of course we avoided thinking about her and Maarten as far as we could. We were masters at avoiding difficult issues. I didn't even want to know her name. A name brings someone closer. Vince rarely spoke it either. Never the wrong name in the heat of the moment, always "Maria".

What a nice bus journey. A private chauffeur for twenty people. Along the dyke, turn off into a village, back onto the dyke. I don't want it to end. On the other side of the window, the world, and not being part of it. No, it was good to see him. It struck me again how easy he is to talk to. The silence he gathers around himself is pleasant; he takes in what I say.

"Maria."

His voice, that hesitant, nasal and slightly dark voice, it was Ishmaël, the letter in his hand. As if he had brought his death sentence to me, so bashful about using my name.

I was proud that he had said it. But I've changed my mind about that since. I forced it too much, was far too eager to understand his life. I was trying to persuade him to step out of the world that was his.

Ishmaël came to me, with that letter, and he simply said "Maria". There's no need for that scene to be as dramatic as I've made it in my mind. My reaction, burying the thing, was actually pretty unnatural too. Even more so than I realised at the time, but I was panicking. I wanted to protect Ishmaël from his past at all costs, from what he'd seen and heard, from the crimes of people like Johnny Kumala.

But it has been nagging away at me. When I told Vince about it, it started to bother me even more that I'd acted so thoughtlessly. That letter could have been key to bringing Kumala to justice. And I wasted it. Why? Panic? Or simply cowardice? I could picture Ishmaël appearing as a witness, going back into his dark past. Boy on the run in another fight with the men who had hunted him. I had to prevent that.

Vince was scared that Elizabeth suspected, maybe even knew. At least he said something along those lines. That it was impossible for him to go on in that twilight of caution and suspicion. We were standing in their kitchen. An impasse – he looked so helpless, he didn't want to go back and he didn't want to go on. All he had learned from his studies appeared to have been forgotten. All he could say to me was that we had to stop seeing each other.

Why, Vince, out of nowhere, after five years of complete surrender?

Everything became stone cold. The house froze around me, him standing there, motionless and so distant, the noise of the gas oven, the quiet buzzing of the fridge, the light of the streetlamp coming through the kitchen window, it was dark, six in the evening, November. Cars along the wet street, my hair still tousled from his embrace.

Elizabeth had been travelling for a few days with a friend, no idea where. The coast was clear, three days going from kitchen to bedroom. They were three days in which he slowly seemed to drift away. He was disappearing, like a thief in the night. He took my soul with him and my heart.

"Maria, we can't keep doing this, I want to, and I love you so much, but we have to stop, we can't go on like this . . ." Vague sounds, I heard what he was saying, the sentences were made up of words and letters, but they had already disintegrated before they reached me.

He did not look at me, had turned his head towards the table with our teacups on, and the previous day's newspaper. The kitchen at its most ordinary, neglected by us, we had only been there briefly to have something to drink.

He sat down, slumped like a sack of potatoes on the kitchen sofa, with its faded upholstery and slightly worn cushions.

Without thinking, he poured cold tea into a cup, stirred it a bit, making little ripples, it sloshed into the saucer, but he didn't notice. He just sat there stirring, silent, looking away, not seeing me. Filled with himself, or empty, that was a possibility, as nothing else came out of him after that last inescapable sentence.

Or out of me.

At that moment, all I wanted to do was go to my piano. Vince has never heard me play. I hardly played in the years we were together. I didn't perform, and I'd stopped teaching too. My hands had their first age spots. God, I was so shocked when I discovered them. Old age begins with your hands.

As he sat there drowning in his tea, I wanted only one thing: my piano. To play, to listen to music that I made myself. The ivory of a key feels so soft. When I'd touched his bare shoulder, still a little chilly from the water, on the little secluded beach where we sometimes went: that is how a piano feels.

After that evening, I started studying again. Every day, Chopin, Schumann, Rachmaninov, mostly those three. I'd like to play them for him. Better than talking maybe, better than all those memories. Ishmaël loved it. Whenever I practised, he was nearby. I'd see him supposedly doing something out on the patio, close to the open window of my room. And then I would play for him.

Just a few more stops, must make sure I don't accidentally miss mine.

I'll tell Vince on Friday about the night Ishmaël appeared at our door. He was having integration classes from Wendy, a big, heavy woman of fifty with a Russian boyfriend, Max, who was twenty years younger and as thin as a rake. An unforgettable duo. Whenever they dropped Ishmaël off at our place in their rickety little car, Maarten said "The Incredible Three" had arrived.

The doorbell rang in the middle of the night. In your sleep, it's like a gunshot going off. Maarten was up and at the door in no time. And there they were. Ishmaël was like a zombie, Wendy had her arm around him, and she pushed him inside. I caught him and led him to my room. He lay down on the couch without a word.

Wendy whispered that Ishmaël had told her he didn't want to go on living. All she could think of to do was to bring him to us. That was the only time he slept at our house.

I asked if he was hungry or thirsty. He shook his head. But he pointed at the piano and placed his hand on his chest.

Then I started playing as I've never played since. Or ever before.

I played him to sleep.

The next day I tried to get him to talk. But he never spoke about it again.

I have to tell this to Vince, exactly like that.

12

Vincent

Friday. That means three days of waiting. She's back. I've pushed her away for so long, for nine years I kept the shutters closed. I have half-lived and half-loved and drifted through the days without a body.

The way we walked to the bus together. I nearly took hold of her hand again.

Her stories shake me up. Everything from before, everything I'd thought was over.

My head is spinning. In Africa with Irene, I drove the Jeep right up to the beach in Dar es Salaam. We got out, walked to the side of the vehicle, slowly sat down on the ground and both leaned back. Her against the front wheel, me against the back wheel, we could just touch hands. We had been on the road for two months, in the interior, two months of dust and mud and potholes and noise. And then suddenly the ocean, the sound of waves.

She said that she felt utterly free, utterly free of worries. She hugged me like never before. We lay weightless in the sand for hours, with some boys playing football nearby.

*

Dar es Salaam, I said the name without even thinking. For a moment, her hospital bed disappeared and she stopped dying. Her face changed instantly, the sound must have taken her to the sea. She was back on our beach.

And I was sitting by her bed and talking to her in that gloomy little hospital where they had taken her when she didn't want any more treatment.

She was my great love for two or three years, the one against which I somehow seemed to measure everything and everybody else.

I never told Maria, but in her arms I was a wingbeat away from Irene. It didn't bother me and I was only half aware of it. How should I put it? She had snared me with her very sophisticated net, hooking me with it, a sort of inner gauze, a soul I hadn't noticed before. Is it possible for someone to return your soul to you?

The soul is such a vague and unsubstantiated concept. Psychologists usually don't go in for it. But I do. That unsubstantiated soul is there, it exists, it is the driving force of your life. Your heart too, but that's a muscle, pumping and piping and finally coming to a stop. But a soul is something else, a soul is over and under everything, like a mist, an invisible connection. Without a soul, you are nowhere, you are a machine, a robot. Someone who attacks villages and chops off heads.

It's just a small step from belief in the soul to belief in God. I never took that step. Even though I sometimes think that it's downright impossible for people simply to exist – or animals, or nature.

Evolution? Absolutely. But who started it, what forces pushed us onward? The laws of an unknowable universe.

I think back to my parents' home. It's Christmas Eve and inside the church it smelled of candles and mandarin peel.

God is homesickness. God is a mandarin.

13

Maria and Vincent

"Hello, Vince."

Careful, don't act too excited, mustn't show I've been counting the hours, slept badly, woke up so early this morning.

Maarten asked me where I was going, which he never does. He spends every day at that genealogical institute now. Recently retired and shutting yourself away all day among old archives and baptism registers and municipal records and goodness knows what other documents. And then in the evening he says: "You know, we're also related to . . .", followed by a name that means nothing to me.

I bet there's not even one woman working out her family tree at that institute. It's an activity for men, for older men. Making a family tree as you approach the end of your life, something to hold onto, so you belong somewhere, and your time will go on. I don't know any women who are interested in family trees, not a single one. It's all a bit childish, all that fuss and nonsense about names and ancestors and distant family and side branches. If you're that interested in branches, go and work in the garden, I said to him once. He thought it was amusing. So did I, truth be told.

*

"Hello, Maria."

Don't hold her hand for too long, just take her coat, don't look at her breasts as she's removing her jacket, don't look at anything, lead the way. Luckily, Elizabeth is already out, and she won't be back until late afternoon. These days she leaves the house early in the morning and doesn't return until the evening. I have no idea what she gets up to. I don't ever ask.

"The days seemed so long, Vince. I hope you don't mind too much that I came to see you. I probably burdened you with all kinds of things. I should apologise."

"No, not at all, if anyone should apologise, it's me. I feel that I said very little to you. But our conversation has been going round inside my head all week. There were so many moments when I should have reacted, but I didn't.

"As we sat there by the river, disturbed by no-one, all I could do was listen and look at the water, hear the ferry coming and going. With you beside me. After all those years. My thoughts were flying in so many directions."

"It really doesn't matter. I felt the same, how could it be otherwise, but I was trying to focus on Ishmaël. You know, it feels so weird to be in your house again. Your room hasn't changed. Where do you want me? Where do your patients sit? Yes, I know. I'm supposed to call them clients."

"I don't have any. I gave up the practice some years ago. It wasn't working so well. I'd turned into some kind of robot, listening, saying something, making notes, then I forgot them again and I started to develop an intense dislike of my profession. Digging and rummaging around in troubled pasts. What was the use? We should all treat our own pasts. I had everyone and his brother bringing me their old neuroses and badly processed experiences – to see if I could quickly sort them all out and defuse them."

"Yes, Vince, you're right, we do have to treat our own pasts. But what is past is not a sickness. Our years together weren't a misfortune. If anything, they were perhaps too happy. I'm shocked to hear you've given up your practice. I hope it was none of my doing."

"Not in the least, Maria. I'm sorry for complaining. When I hear you talking about Ishmaël, my frustration with psychology diminishes. Curiously, it even reconciles me to it a little.

"But sit down, I'll try to be more useful. Why don't you tell me about the day when Ishmaël disappeared?"

"I will do my best. It's so odd that I didn't see it coming. I didn't suspect a thing. I thought we had made our lives fit a certain daily rhythm. He arrived at eight o'clock, took the newspaper out of the letterbox, brought it to the house, said hello to us, walked to his little shed at the end of the garden to make his ginger tea, and waited to see if Maarten or I had anything in mind for the day. His presence was somehow soothing.

"Maarten says it was because of him. Yes, you look surprised, and I can see why. I haven't told you that Maarten had also become very attached to Ishmaël over the years. He was crazy about him, called him Ish, went out with him, was proud of him. I found it difficult at times. It stopped just short of jealousy. I understood it from Ishmaël's point of view, that he thought a man was more important. He had grown up with the idea that men are in charge. I don't think Maarten wanted to come between me and Ishmaël, but he was drawn to the boy, he was glad he was there. He was the only one who had an easy time making him laugh. I watched them sometimes, digging out stones or cutting down a tree in the garden. Before Ishmaël came, Maarten didn't spend a single minute there. One day they tried to fix the front tyre of my bicycle. It was summer, they were sitting on the drive, clumsy, unsure how to proceed. Maarten mending a tyre, I thought. Now I've seen it all. I overheard him explaining how you have to remove it with a sort of fork, and then locate the puncture using a bucket of water. Ishmaël looked at him in despair, and then suddenly Maarten took the bucket and tipped it over his own head. I'd never seen Ishmaël laugh like that. Maarten splashed the last of the water at him, and he jumped aside and laughed even louder. A warm summer's day, there was not a cloud in the sky, not then . . .

"And then the day came when Ishmaël was going to get his Dutch passport. I'd worked towards it with him for years, into one government agency and out of another, into a language class, out of an assimilation course, into the embassy, out of a consulate, forms, applications, hours on the telephone, visits to the town hall, such a vast amount of paperwork.

"Don't ever get that involved, Vince, never say to someone: I'll help you to get a passport, it's one long exercise in discouragement from every branch of officialdom.

"But anyway, at long last, there came a message that Ishmaël's passport was ready. They organise a special event for the occasion. The mayor gives a speech for the new Dutch citizens, and there's a ceremonial presentation of the passports.

"But not for Ishmaël. He hadn't told us he could go and collect his passport, and he hadn't gone to the ceremony either. He'd gone to pick it up on a weekday. As we later discovered.

"I called the council at some point, and they told me the passport had been issued to Mr Bah two weeks before.

"I thought it was very odd. So I asked Ishmaël if he'd like to bring his passport round, so that we could celebrate together. He said he didn't have it.

"So I got angry with the civil servant, who had obviously looked up the wrong Bah. I called again and got the same answer: Mr Bah had already collected it.

"Then Maarten said to him that he really should show us his passport, and then we could all give him three cheers. Those were his exact words: 'give him three cheers'.

"That was on a Friday – Ishmaël said he'd bring it with him on Monday and, yes, he'd just received it.

"And that Monday he didn't turn up. Maarten had stayed at home, he was so eager to take a photograph of Ishmaël with the passport in his hand. Bureaucracy defeated, time to make up for those lost years, the escape and the danger were over, hurrah for Holland, hurrah for everyone who had helped, hurrah for our Ishmaël Bah. But there was no Ish coming up the drive, holding out his hand to greet Bijke. And not in the days after that either. The days turned into weeks and months. He never did come back.

"Maarten still keeps insisting that it's all his fault. But he's just saying that for my sake. It's not his fault at all.

"In the days leading up to it all, there was nothing unusual going on, nothing alarming, no indication whatsoever. Ishmaël reacted very calmly to the passport issue too. The calm before the storm, a storm we didn't understand, didn't want, could not have foreseen."

"Of course, I went to his home. The hours I waited near his house! The blinds were always closed. Not even a strip of light coming through in the evening. He didn't respond to the doorbell, I knocked on his door, called his name, I asked his downstairs neighbour if she ever heard him walking around.

"Yes, in the past, she'd heard water from what must have been a shower. But not lately. No, she hadn't seen him for the past few weeks, no, she hadn't ever seen him, only heard him. But that made sense, because she worked at night and slept in the daytime.

"He simply wasn't there anymore.

"For weeks, I kept going to his place at all kinds of hours. I knew he sometimes went to a bar to watch sports, even though he had a T.V. of his own. But I didn't dare to go and look for him there, afraid of finding him with people he knew, afraid he might run away, or ignore me, or, well, you know, you imagine all manner of things. And what right did I have to bother him when he was sitting peacefully in a bar?

"I forced myself not to do anything else. He'd come back. I was sure of it, Vince. At the time.

"Maarten believes Ishmaël may have supposed we wanted to trick him out of his passport. It's a ridiculous idea, but perhaps there's something to it.

"Maybe he suddenly got scared. That the only thing in his life that had worked out would be taken from him. Just as everything, his family, his village, had been taken, dragged off, wiped out, murdered. But not by Maarten or by me! How could he think that after all those years?"

14

Vincent and Maria

Five years. And then we put a stop to our love. Turning away, fleeing, from one day to the next. Away from the indescribable space of our illicit love. Five years of adventure, travelling, on a night train through a hidden world. Where you laughed and danced and sat in a bar until late, on your way to a new memory.

She is still so beautiful and so familiar. Her story about Ishmaël leaving is like mine. I abandoned her in the same way. But she still had Ishmaël, and I had no-one. I remained behind in my love for her, which I had blown to pieces.

I went on loving her stubbornly, continuously. I drove to her house at night a few times. Down the dyke along the river, through her village, up the road to their rural neighbourhood. Sometimes I saw light in their rooms from a distance. But more often it was dark, just one light by a shed. Like some sort of highwayman, I stood in the bushes by the path to their property. In the middle of the night, I just waited there, frozen, silent.

It was all my own fault.

It obviously makes no sense for Maarten to take the blame.

That nice Maarten, who I talked to twice. Once in Stockholm, and later that time in Utrecht, in very different circumstances. Although you couldn't really call it talking. It was a profound silence.

We were walking through Utrecht, she and I, sometimes hand in hand, cautiously. He must have seen it. He came out of a side street of the Janskerkhof, where it was busy and we had thought no-one would notice us. We knew he was in Utrecht though. They had come together. Maarten was there for work.

It was cold, and we were walking through the flower market on the square. I had taken hold of her hand and put it in my jacket pocket, trying to warm her icy fingers. She pulled herself away and walked towards him, smiling, enthusiastic.

Maarten looked at me. He said hello, gave me a nod, they talked for a minute. He looked at me again, raised a hand. He seemed so defenceless.

That never-forgotten afternoon, we were as dumbstruck as Maarten. Does she still remember it, does she still remember it all? I do, every one of the days of our years together. When you add up all those days, you get no more than three full months that we were together, elevated above the rest of time.

There's that puzzling pain in my neck again, that cramp. An unpleasant sensation.

"What is it? You're pale. Shall I get you some water? No, wait, I know where it is. You stay there."

Her hand with the glass of water. I feel fine now. The pain's gone already. Worrying about nothing. Alright, I'll drink it.

"Thank you, that's kind, but it's nothing serious. But this is not about me, it's about you. Your last days with Ishmaël. They remind me so very much of our own last days together. Elizabeth away somewhere travelling with a friend, the two of us finally alone, days to ourselves. I had known the time was coming, I had been looking forward to it for weeks, I couldn't wait for Elizabeth to leave."

"No, Vince, don't go on, stop. There's no point."

"I need to explain it to you. I cannot stop now. For so long, I've . . . Listen, give me a few minutes."

"But it's not really why we're here . . ."

"That's true, we're here because you came to me. Because of the way you feel after what happened with Ishmaël, of course, but I think it has just as much to do with us. And you know that too, or you'd never have called me. I'm so very glad you did. I was afraid I would never see you again."

"No, not now, Vince, not even for a moment. You already feel too close. Can I come back another time? Next week? Wednesday at four, O.K? I promise I'll be there."

15

Maria

I don't know if it's a good idea to go and see him again. I've already said so much and what else do I really have to say? Vince wants to talk about us, of course. He was a bit out of sorts, he seemed slow somehow, not quite himself.

He drank the water I gave him like a child. His hand around mine, his pleasant hand. I was afraid it would begin again, that I would go astray. But it didn't happen, my body did not react, his touch did not trigger anything.

Had I come to him to talk about us? He was determined to believe that I had. I have to admit he felt very close, and the old days did come back to me.

I saw his longing and his regret and his uneasiness. I almost felt a kind of pity, if I'm honest. Am I honest? I'm not so sure about that. Honesty – what is it? Sometimes it's just a rod for the back of the person you live with.

No, I will go. I promised him and it felt strange, the way we said goodbye. I can't really cancel at the last minute. I'll leave a note for Maarten, tell him I'll be home at half-past six.

*

It's nice to be sitting on the bus, in this rain. Those poor cyclists on the dyke, heading into the wind. That's where Ishmaël and I turned left on the rare occasion when he didn't walk over and we cycled into town together. He did have a bike, but he preferred to walk. A little slowly, even a little subdued, as if he were hesitating. As if he were not actually allowed to be walking there, as if he were not there at all.

I saw him walk up and down our drive hundreds of times, I watched him as he walked away beneath the trees along the lane, always on the road next to the kerb, never on the pavement. Gym shoes, black trousers, a jacket and, when he'd been to the barber, a baseball cap. He was suddenly almost bald, and his usual head of curls looked so good on him.

In the first year, he sometimes limped as he walked up the drive, and one time his arm was in a sling. Looked as if he'd been fighting. He mumbled something about a fall.

There were rival groups of Sierra Leoneans in the Netherlands at the time, so one of the newspapers said. I often wondered if Ishmaël was involved. Had he been attacked? He spent a lot of time talking on the telephone, always in Fula. From a distance, I watched him making agitated gestures.

I couldn't imagine it. He was so gentle, he avoided any form of aggression. And who would ever want to harm him?

Later, when slowly but surely he began to take up his place in our life, I heard him one time on the telephone saying:

Mi yidi ma, "I love you." I recognised those words, as I had asked Ishmaël how to say that in his language.

I repeated them to him with a smile. He nodded.

He was not much of a cyclist. He didn't put out his hand to signal, because then he would lose his balance. He was forever swerving, just a little, and he struggled to take bends. Clumsy, small, slow and so very, very sweet. I miss him so much.

During my first attempts to find him, I had to describe him. A young man from Sierra Leone in a baseball cap, jacket, black trousers. There are quite a few of those, the neighbour I spoke to said, the one who knew him only from the sound of his shower. Describing someone is an art.

I tried again, saying: "He looks a bit like a young Michael Jackson." Bless her, I could see the woman thinking. How do you describe someone you miss and why it is that you miss them?

I miss him, I don't know quite what that means. It was the same when Vince left me. But the feeling was so intense that I thought I would never be able to love anyone or anything ever again.

I have to get off the bus.

Why do I feel so wretched and miserable about a boy who went his own way without looking back? What did I expect from Ishmaël? Just leave him be. He doesn't belong to me. A nice line to walk through the rain with: Leave him be, doesn't belong to me. Leave him be, doesn't belong to me. Will it help if I sing that song for ten minutes, all the way to Vince's door? Maybe then I can coolly say to him, "Never mind, Vince, I've just walked Ishmaël out of my system." Wouldn't he be surprised? Walking as therapy. Maybe that's not such a bad idea.

God, this wind! I didn't used to have any difficulty walking, but I can already feel it in my legs.

"Those who make their own way through the world hear one day their own song in life." Who's that by, Vince?

I cannot believe I ever fell for such an unpoetic man.

Walking along to sentences and fragments: "I went to Bommel to see the bridge." "Gone, gone, oh, gone for good." "The rains that hung between us, Claudien, are over and the night is white."

This rain – will it never stop? I'm going to be soaked through by the time I get there. Shelter for a moment. No, keep walking, the church clock says it's already quarter past four. But it's been ten minutes fast for years.

Keep going. Don't stop. A stop light for pedestrians in the rain and there are no cars or bikes around. As if anyone would stop then, but I still see people doing it. I don't.

The 1930s neighbourhood where he lives somehow suits him, roads with lots of trees, the houses set a little apart. I can already see the house he paid off by listening. He always laughed when I said that.

16

Vincent

Ten past four. She should be ringing the doorbell any moment now. She doesn't wear a watch, but she has an inner clock, she's always on time. It's raining, and if she took the bus, then the bus must be late.

Elizabeth left the house so early this morning, and she comes home later every day. I have no idea what she's up to. She's in a good mood, though. She was singing the other day and clearly felt shy when I came into the room and heard her. She's got a beautiful voice, practises a lot with her choir. Everyone seems to be joining choirs these days.

I hear something, a car door closing. It is Wednesday today, isn't it? I think we said four. Can't imagine I wrote it down wrong. I didn't need to make a note, because my entire week was directed towards it, but I still put it in my diary to be on the safe side. Yes, there it is.

An old reflex, in order to make everything look right, all the paperwork needs to be just so, in case anyone asks later where you were at such and such a time.

Back then, with Maria, I wrote clients I didn't even have into my diary, I made up names, it was an urge to make the days look normal. Then I felt that my tracks were covered. If Elizabeth looked at my diary, she'd just think I was working. So I could go and see Maria without anyone thinking it out of the ordinary. Self-deception, it made no sense. I eventually ended up with an entire parallel programme of activities.

What's the best way to tell her that Ishmaël will never come back? I'll have to be so careful, so clear. To tell her that, as far as Ishmaël is concerned, she is a station he has passed through. Has he gone back to Freetown, is that possible? With a Dutch passport, he has no need to be afraid, he can come and go at any time.

But no, he hasn't gone back. Back is not what a refugee wants. Back is an outdated concept, back is poverty, back is terror. Away, ahead, forwards, not backwards.

She must be ill. But she would have let me know. Traffic jam, car's broken down, she could call me. She's not coming, it's quarter past four, she's not coming again. But maybe something's happened.

I probably frightened her off. I was far too open with her. Damn it, I said the wrong thing. No wonder she's gone, she got scared. She's told Maarten. She's told him all about us, sworn that it's firmly in the past, finished forever. She's back to her old self, she just wants to know how Ishmaël is doing. As long as somehow she gets to hear he's alive, how he's living, where.

And that nice Maarten will have kept silent, just as he

did on that day in Utrecht. He had known for a long time, but he simply got over it, without apportioning blame, without aggression.

I don't understand why she hasn't sent me a message.

Mercifully, Elizabeth doesn't bother with me. She leaves me in peace, does her own thing.

And why has my father been in my room so often these past few days? There's no-one I have loved more than my father, not even Maria.

But that's not love, that's something else, my father is something other than words.

He ties the sledge behind our car, the snow on the roads is deep. Very carefully, he pulls me along, faster and faster. The road leads to the woods, I'm seven years old, eight at most, the pine trees above me, the white cloud from the exhaust pipe, the sound of the engine. I can see his hat through the rear window, I'm on the sledge as if in the palm of a giant hand.

Ever since then, he has been pulling me along, he is my engine, he is a hand. A limitless feeling, even though it is a thing of the past, something from which I have never been able to detach myself.

Let the world perish, and it will, but I don't care. Once my father was here, he existed, he lived, he talked to me, taught me words.

17

Vincent and Maria

"Maria! I was afraid you weren't going to come. You're soaked. Aren't you cold? Would you like me to fetch you a jumper?

"I've spent the past few days half in a dream, every hour lasted a day. Thinking so much about you and about us. When you were twenty minutes late, I started imagining all kinds of things.

"But I couldn't stop thinking about your story about Ishmaël either. It felt as if he came so very close to me, stiflingly so. A boy on the run, from a part of the world you don't know anything about and don't want to know anything about.

"I couldn't help thinking that you only told me the whole story about Ishmaël to show me that I'm like him. I too suddenly disappeared. It's probably an occupational hazard, ideas from my old practice. But whatever it is, whether you meant something by it or not, Ishmaël's story has really been on my mind this week.

"You'll think it's foolish, but I looked out for him on the streets, I thought I saw him go into a café. I saw him walking along in his black trousers, gym shoes, jacket and a baseball cap.

"It's been the same with you these past years. I would see you in a line of people in front of the cinema. Or on a bus or walking through a supermarket.

"I'm sorry for ambushing you like this. You haven't even sat down yet. Here, take this chair. That's where I always sat when I had clients."

"I spent nine years talking to you, in my head and sometimes out loud, here, in this room, when Elizabeth wasn't at home. All those years, I imagined how you were living, what you were doing.

"I abandoned you. But I don't need to tell you that, do I? At the time, fear was stronger than love. I didn't dare to face the chaos that would follow if our relationship came to light. Which was bound to happen. Maybe it had already happened though, that day when Elizabeth appeared in the kitchen and gave me that look of concern, of suspicion.

"I took what had grown over the course of five years and pulled it out of the ground.

"Then I started to imagine that it was you who left me. Sometimes I was sure of it, that it was you who didn't want to see me anymore, that I was too much of a threat. It's the world turned upside down, I know. But somehow it got me through each day.

"So two years ago, I decided to give up my practice, to put a stop to the masquerade that had been going on all those years, playing the exhausting role of a therapist with his clients. Since I let you go, no matter where I was, I've never really felt that I was in the right place. I did everything I could to hide the fact that I had nothing to hold onto, no balance. My balance, my rock, had been you.

"And then, when I saw your name on my screen two weeks ago, I couldn't believe my eyes! If I hadn't answered, would you have thought I wasn't around anymore, had changed my number, moved house, something like that?

"But of course I answered. I was overjoyed."

"Steady, Vince. My reason for coming today was to tell you that I am not going to see you anymore. Last week I realised that we were starting to, well, you know, see if we could – I noticed it in everything, especially in myself. I don't want to talk to you anymore about Ishmaël, or about us. I'm sorry. But you really helped me, probably without realising it."

"Helped you? I hardly said anything. I only started talking to you once you had gone."

"All week I've been reliving those years with you, Vince. A real sense of longing for that incredible time together. It undermined the foundations of my life, but somehow became part of it. I don't know how, but it seems that I have the ability to take even the very worst things that happen to me and twist them around, so that I can go on. Now that I've realised that, I can move on. Honestly. It was important for me to speak to you. I saw you and heard you and understood you.

"You did the right thing, you know, putting a stop to it.

Otherwise we would only have found ourselves sooner or later in an impossible predicament. We were tied to other people, on all sides, and they wouldn't have let go. Not Maarten, not Elizabeth, and not the children.

"Bringing our relationship to an end was the best thing you could have done. When you let me leave the house, and go out into that cold and rainy night, I knew at once that our love had somehow been saved. An open ending. We had both stayed where we belonged. The distance you put between us gave me space. I could remain close to you, without anyone knowing.

"I could start loving you again, just like I used to, but strangely that's no longer necessary. What we had is still there. There's nothing to add, nothing to prove. We haven't forgotten each other. We are here."

"Did I mention, Vince, that I've started studying piano again? A higher form of disappearance. My years at the conservatory came back to me, the hours of practice. It brought the house to life. Maybe I started playing so that I didn't have to think.

"Even now I'd rather be playing something for you than talking. My thoughts can't keep up with my feelings. When my mother died, a friend of mine played a piece by Liszt, 'Liebestraum'. Do you know it?"

"Yes. A few simple notes, but they can conjure up such an enigmatic sense of melancholy. A beautiful piece. Sadly I don't have a piano, or I'd have asked you to play it for me."

"When I play, I forget everything around me. With good

music, you're the one who is played, swept along, the sound does its work, and as a pianist you don't have to do much more than press the keys at the right moment. No need to think about it, it just happens, you're part of the music, your hands are an extension of the notes. Floating along like a swimmer in the current of a river. Yes, that's it, you float along. Like our years together, Vince."

"Maria, don't laugh, please, hear me out. I've been thinking about this all week, and I can't get it out of my head. I told you that I've felt Ishmaël's presence over the past few days. That sounds pretty dramatic, I know. But it's true. His story, and ours, they're somehow connected. If we'd kept going, you would never have felt the freedom you needed to let him into your life.

"So now for the question that's been on my mind constantly for the past few days. Would you mind if I made an attempt to find Ishmaël for you? I have a strong feeling I could track him down – I have to. Not to persuade him to go back to you and Maarten, but to find out how he's doing, if he needs any help. Maybe it's an impractical plan, but, as I said, I can't get it out of my mind."

"But what if you find him? What then?"

"Then at least we'll know he's alive and out there somewhere. And you won't be in this constant state of uncertainty. It might even give you back your old life. From before Ishmaël, from before me."

"From before you? Do you really think that would be possible? Realigning the stars? No, no, our years can't be turned back or changed, at most they only alter our loneliness, the way a poem sometimes can.

"My memory, my body, my whole way of thinking, my soul, you subtly shifted them in your direction, changing my course. I don't know a better way to put it."

"Just as you say, that's exactly how it happened. I can hear myself when you talk like that. It took me almost nine years to realise that I belong with no-one else but you.

"All those people who used to come and see me, they were looking for one and the same thing: to be at home somewhere. A concept from a mythical world, not designed or dreamed by anyone, a cry from Paradise: home. It comes from the nursery of our memory.

"You talked about poems that change loneliness, and when we stopped seeing each other, I started reading poetry. The work was a revelation, to be honest. I never knew any of the poets you mentioned, but now I know them all. It felt as if I was bringing you back. I read and read and read. In part so that I didn't have to think of you."

"Your plan doesn't sound feasible, Vince. It's an idiotic undertaking. Where would you even begin? I've tried everything myself, but he's nowhere. No-one knows where he is. Maybe he did go back to Sierra Leone, who can say? He didn't seem to have any friends here, didn't know the neighbours. I searched and searched, but at a certain point it became problematic. I felt as if I was some kind of detective. What right did I have to him? Why did I think I could just go chasing after him?"

"I'm not going to chase after him, Maria, that's not the idea. I'm just convinced that it would allow me to put something right. It would be good for you if I could track him down. So let me try."

"Alright then, Vince, fine, I can't stop you. Try to find him. I hope you succeed. But don't ask him to come back to us, you have to let him go. If he wants to come back himself, I'll be delighted, of course. But even if I just find out how he's doing, then I can start looking forward again."

"Forward? All I want to do is go back."

"That's impossible, Vince, as you know."

"You're right. But between knowing and wanting, there is a battlefield."

"Says the old psychologist."

"Hmm. Old?"

"Well, a good bit younger than me, but still old."

"Young enough to take your hand and . . ."

"Oh, sorry, Vince. Maarten's calling, I should have turned off my mobile. I need to go."

Part 2

1

Maria

A memory casually blowing in and out again, for almost sixty years now. How old was I, six, seven? I can see two bridges, their long arms reaching across a vast stretch of water. The Moerdijkbrug, the railway bridge, as I later learned. Water everywhere, slowly rising higher and higher. We're sitting on a green strip of land, which is suddenly surrounded. Our picnic things lie all around, looking pretty forlorn. My father and mother are trying to talk some sense into each other, their hands clutching the folding chairs we brought. My brother and I, we're looking at them, at the water, at the grey sky above us. My brother's already a good swimmer, but I am not.

My father says I'm going to have to climb onto his back. I can feel the tension, see the piece of land around us getting smaller. The water's going to be all over our picnic any minute. But where can we go? Everything's so far away.

Then my mother and father start waving like crazy, with a towel, with a hat, and shouting. In the distance, a boat sails past with people on it, who wave back. And that's all they do. But then, the next moment, the boat's there, up close. We wade through the water, someone throws a rope towards us, they pull us up, I shout that we've forgotten my book, but everything's already floating. I see my mother crying and laughing.

A lucky escape, we are told. It was pure chance that the boat came past. We'd never have made it without them.

It's quiet. I've noticed that I've started talking out loud to myself more and more these days. When there's no-one else at home, no-one except for Bijke. Talking to your dog, it happens automatically. Is that the start of the downward slope? Maybe a dog is better than a psychologist, it's certainly cheaper. Bijke's a good listener, and she sometimes gives you an unexpected shake of the paw too. Like a person really, no, softer than a person. I remember how Ishmaël avoided Bijke at first, wary of her persistent attention. But in time he made peace with her and took her out for long and happy walks. Two listeners, they were, natural allies. Bijke looked miserable for weeks after Ishmaël disappeared.

Where's Vince? He was going to call me when he got back from Florence. There was a conference for psychologists, and he had no business being there really, but an American friend of his was going, someone he had not seen for a long time.

He should have been home almost a week by now. Or is he waiting until we see each other tomorrow? Tomorrow, at five. He persuaded me to go round there one more time.

Or have I got it wrong? Has he only just got back?

Has he found out anything about Ishmaël yet? I can't imagine that he has, or I'd have heard from him. I don't understand why he was so persistent, the way he talked me round. He seemed determined that he was going to look for Ishmaël. Was it because of me, so that he wouldn't have to let me go? Was it because I had said I did not want to see him again?

When exactly did it all begin, getting closer, falling in love – and how and why? Now it almost seems like a mystery, but then it was crystal clear, it was there from the moment we got talking. Funnily enough, it happened in a harbour, just like later in Stockholm. It was on a boat, where we were celebrating Vera and Julius's silver wedding anniversary. I hadn't seen Vince since our sensitivity session, or even thought about him. I had no idea that he knew our friends, or rather Maarten's friends.

The party boat had a number of decks, with bars and dancefloors and with velvet and brass all over the place, and fake paintings on the walls. Chairs around chessboards, bridge corners, a reading table. Married for twenty-five years, a marathon. Vera and Julius were walking around with numbers on their backs and laurel wreaths on their heads like Romans who had won a race. Their best man and bridesmaids, who had been drummed up for the occasion, had come up with the idea one boozy afternoon.

"Twenty-five years." Vince gave a loud sigh and shook his

head. I couldn't help laughing at his tragicomic act. His hair was quite long, and he was wearing a linen jacket, green shoes and a watch with a green strap. My first impression was that he thought too much about his clothes: vain. Second impression was that it looked borderline scruffy. Maybe he wasn't so vain after all.

The top deck was almost deserted, and there was dancing downstairs. On the reading table, there were just empty glasses, no newspapers. A couple of people at the bar, a ceiling fan wafting a bit of cool air around. Funny how some scenes and events cannot be erased, how they lie there waiting under the surface, razor sharp, every detail visible. Is it like that for everyone?

It was warm, the end of June, summer holidays on the way, children's end-of-year exams over – it was break time for everyone. Does he still remember? Of course he does, we've repeated it all so often. The first time this, the first time that . . .

"Don't think, Maria," he said the first time he undressed me and I hesitated to lean in to his embrace, mumbling something like "I don't think it's a good idea to . . ." Don't think.

I remember wandering around the boat a bit aimlessly, Maarten had joined some people at a bridge table. The happy couple loved games of all kinds and had kindly provided a variety of ways to pass the time. Chess, bridge, ping-pong, shuffleboard, boules, darts, billiards, mah-jong, roulette, life was a continuous game for them.

*

"Twenty-five years of playing cards and gambling, sounds like fun." Those were his first words, followed by that sigh about being married for twenty-five years, and then, "So, Maria, do you still work at that place?"

He pulled up two chairs to the reading table and we sat down. Bridge takes hours, so I had time. I hadn't worked there for a long time and I started telling him about what I had been doing and what I did and what I wanted to do in the future.

He was a relative stranger, though. A man who, long ago, had infiltrated our office and broken it apart with all his sensitivity.

Later on, I told him about the failed music career I had had before ending up at that strange office. He laughed when he heard I had plucked up the courage to walk out of the rehearsal for a concert we were supposed to be giving that same eve-ning. Such a commotion. I can still remember how much Vince enjoyed the story. The conductor had already roared at me a few times for not paying attention, but he was the one who kept coming in too late. I stood up, pushed back my piano stool, apparently very calm, and slammed the lid shut with as much sang-froid as I could muster. The crack of a whip, cutting straight through the conductor's yelling. I looked at the man for a second, waved to the orchestra and headed straight for the dressing room. Never to return.

As we shared those small stories about our lives, we started looking at each other a little longer. I hadn't talked like that to a man for ages. Even the silences were enjoyable.

We listened to each other, like children having stories read to them in bed. Wrapped up in a sort of conspiracy. Nothing and no-one ready to pounce; everything happened effortlessly, endlessly.

Our cautious approach began then, the slow growth of familiarity. I very clearly remember sensing the danger.

Because of his uninhibited questions, his bold, almost wild way of looking, of his hands and voice. His eyes.

I can still hear the thrum and hum of the party on the lower deck, now and then a few people came and joined us in the bar. A handful hung around, but most left pretty quickly, it was too quiet there, too empty.

When the boat bumped against the quay and an oompah band paraded around the rooms followed by a long line of party-goers, we realised a whole evening had gone by. Party over. We went home, with a premonition of some new restlessness.

Maarten said with a grin that he'd been playing bridge on the bridge, and that there had been prizes. He wanted to know where I'd been and what I'd done. Oh, I just wandered around, bit of a chat here and there, no-one in particular. It was how my shadow life began, with an evasive answer to the very first question.

Maarten and I – we hit our own silver twenty-fifth long ago. How everything became as it is, a life with him and our children – at a certain point it all becomes a blur. It grows, without any specific intention, expanding, the sun rising and setting, the tides coming in and going out, the wind rising and falling. You move, alone and together, for so many years.

No, I'm not leaving, of course not, here in this house is where I have to stay, I wouldn't know how to live if I were to leave here.

It was so very different with Maarten than with Vince. Maarten calm, balanced, forgiving, with a deep dislike of conflict. Vince quick, exciting, and so good at putting himself in other people's shoes.

I had to trick Maarten into taking me out. And it was me who kissed him first, or nothing would ever have happened. There are times when I'd like to stop our film there. We never mentioned it again in this curious life of ours. Not a bad life, not at all, but strange. And sometimes disconcerting, the way you're no longer sure how it all came about and why we married and had children and, maybe later, grandchildren.

I wonder if Maarten ever thinks back to it. How I reeled him in, without his seeming to notice, without him resisting. He always reacted so seriously, so shyly, cautiously.

Our last year at the conservatory. Everyone had already left the room where we had been practising. Seven of us were going on a small tour, strings, wind section and me on the piano. Maarten still played the cello back then, more beautifully than anyone I knew. I never understood why he decided to give it up. He simply left and found a job that had nothing to do with music. All in that simple, imperturbable way of his. He didn't think he was good enough.

I'm sure that influenced me later when I so abruptly stopped playing.

He walked over to me, holding his cello. I was still at the piano, trying out a new piece. And he asked if I'd help him with a stuck tuning peg or something. He was almost standing to attention, with his cello in one hand, close to the piano, waiting, a loyal musical soldier, ready to play if required.

We had had supper the previous evening, and the week before too, every week, in fact, for a few months. I stood up, almost brushing against him, and went to take his cello. He smiled, and then I kissed him, as if it had to be. Without surrender, without fear. I kissed his mouth, for a moment, and then his eyes. And he simply stood there, motionless, said not a word. He put down the cello and, in a daze, sat down unthinkingly on the bass keys of the piano, for which he immediately apologised. I started laughing, and that's when he took me in his arms.

That is where it should have stopped, the film, right there. There could be no better ending. But it was the beginning.

Seeing Vince again, talking to him, about Ishmaël and about us, makes it feel as if I'm gradually getting back on track. I have to confess that his listening helped, even though I didn't think it would and had little hope when I called him. It was a bizarre leap of faith, a last resort, a reckless act. His voice, his name on the telephone, my heart was thumping so hard I thought he could hear it on the other end of the line.

Was it really because of Ishmaël that I called him? Yes, that too. But I think my longing to see him at least once more was what lay behind the whole venture. The years without him, nine whole years, I endured them, and Ishmaël took his place to a certain extent, but I didn't want to die without ever seeing Vince again. Oh heavens, I'm rambling on and on.

2

Maria and Elizabeth

I didn't know travelling on a bus could be so soothing. This is the third time recently that I've come along this dyke. Look, down there, that's where we sat a couple of weeks ago. There's a group of cyclists at our table now.

Us, we. I'm instinctively thinking in the plural again.

The light on the water reminds me of Terschelling. It was the beginning of October. We were both able to get away for a weekend. Maarten was travelling for work, and I can't remember where Elizabeth was.

The island was pretty much deserted. We walked along an empty beach, rode along shell paths to the Brandaris lighthouse and leaned our bikes against a wall beside the café. The ferry from Harlingen was just coming in beneath us. We could still sit outside, the sun was warm. Indian summer, the days were snipped out of the season, you could not tell if it was summer or autumn.

We sat there, We sat there, light and light-hearted. He was boyish, kept kissing me. I tried gently to fend him off, warned him to be careful. "You never know, Vince."

"What if I gave up my practice and we went to live in

Italy?" he said out of the blue. I had no idea where that came from. But just as recklessly, I said I thought it was a wonderful idea.

On an island, everything seems possible. On a bright day in October, when the world has transformed into a meaningful whole, then you say "yes".

We had never been closer. I don't think I ever loved him more.

It was the first time he'd spoken about stopping work. He wasn't really happy with what he was doing. There was always a vague restlessness in him. Sometimes he distrusted his own profession. Even though he was obviously so good. The way he encouraged me to talk, with just a few simple questions. And the loving attention he had devoted to Ishmaël.

When I see him later, I'll tell him that the two weeks he was away have had a good effect, and that I can go it alone from here, that I feel much better. We mustn't see each other again. Not go back into that shadow, that double life.

"Don't think, Maria."

Oh, but I will. Not thinking gave me years of happiness, that's true, but now I can't stop thinking. I've become afraid of that overwhelming feeling, of that love of ours. I can't do it anymore, and my body's become old, it would take fright.

It's such beautiful weather. Every time the bus doors open, the scent of freshly mown grass wafts in. Vince will have had a good time in Italy, if it wasn't too hot. He thinks twenty degrees is more than enough. Hardly suited to Italy then.

I'm nice and early this time. So I can walk there. The clock's striking five. A church bell in a quiet neighbourhood, in the summer, I count the strokes, time contracts. My parents are alive again, now, they're in the house, I'm playing on the street, riding my bike to the swimming baths, sailing a rubber dinghy along the canal behind our house, sitting in our Renault Quatre again.

It was our first car. Beige, a sort of beetle, with the engine at the back. Scarcely enough room for one suitcase in the front. We had a rack on top for holidays, a sort of detachable luggage rack. Going to Luxembourg was an epic journey.

His house. It's so peaceful here. Funny, a whole line of flowers at the window of his office. I've never seen flowers in his room before. Does he have something to celebrate?

The bell's so loud, I've never noticed that before.

"Hello, I'm Elizabeth, we met once, a long time ago. You had an appointment with Vince, didn't you? I saw it in his diary."

"Yes, hello, yes, that's right. Can't he make it?"

"I'm really sorry to tell you, out here on the doorstep like this, but Vince passed away. Very suddenly. At the airport in Rome. He was on his way home. I didn't have an address for you, or I would have written to you. We buried him the day before yesterday.

"And we found a letter in his luggage addressed to a Maria. Do you think it might be you?"

Keep standing upright, just don't cry with Elizabeth here. His heart, of course. He was always prepared for it, took all kinds of pills, but didn't want to worry anyone, no-one else needed to know that he was at risk of sudden death. I knew, and I was often worried, but nothing ever happened. It was under control, and the miracle pills were guarding the fort, so he claimed. When he went pale the other day, I foolishly didn't give it a thought.

"Come on in, you can sit in his room, I'll be back in a second." The accoutrements of his daily life: his letter opener on the desk, so old-fashioned in the days of smartphones, stacks of books leaning against his desk, the floor lamp with a business card clipped to its shade, a stuffed crow in the corner next to a metal rubbish bin painted with birds – "my aviary" – the two chairs opposite each other, always in conversation, a wooden tennis racquet on the wall, the photographs of his parents, a faded poster of the piazza in Siena.

"They say it's the most beautiful square in the world, Maria. It's built in the centre of the town in the shape of a shell. We must go there one day." A shell. As a child, you held them up to your ear so you could hear the sea.

Oh, there's someone else in the house, a woman's voice in the hallway, saying something kind to Elizabeth. It's good that someone's with her. I should give her my condolences and tell her how sorry I am for her loss. She looked sad, but not defeated.

It must be a mistake, you'll be home any minute, it's a joke, a trap. Why am I here, Vince? I didn't know, I was mowing the grass while they were burying you. You can't have been buried, that's impossible.

She's taking such a long time to fetch that letter. There's no way Vince would have written to me, he hadn't done that for a long time, just at the beginning.

Yes, I can clearly hear them talking now, Elizabeth and another woman.

"You have to let her see the letter, Elizabeth, it's got her name on it."

"But it could be someone else, another Maria."

"Just give it to her. She'll know if it's meant for her."

It's for me, he didn't know any other Marias, give me the letter, and then I can leave.

"I think this is for you. Is that likely? Could you just open it, please?"

It's a letter to me. D.M., it says at the top, he always wrote that, D.M. They're just notes, seems like a kind of diary. He's talking to me.

"Thank you, yes, yes, it's for me, he's writing about the problems I came to see him for. I haven't even offered you my condolences. What a shock it must have been for you. I'd just like you to know how sorry I am. It's all so unexpected. May I ask you where he was buried?"

"In Rome. He bought a plot there years ago. Thank you for your sympathy. I hope he was able to be a help to you."

He has been with her all these years, every day and night. She's still attractive, but reserved somehow. Deliberately formal with me. Does she suspect? She's not showing any sign of it. She is strong, guarded, so very different from Vince.

Rome. You once talked to me about it, Vince, the eternal city, said that one day you would like to live there.

3

Maria

The late sun, the roads are so quiet. I have to go to the bus stop, but I think I'm walking the wrong way. No, it's alright, there's the church.

The bells are chiming again. So I was there a whole hour. They insisted on offering me something to drink. Sadly, I didn't catch the name of the friend who brought the tea and stayed with us, though I'm glad she did. We sat there together, a little awkward, cautious, the three of us in his room. It wasn't unpleasant, but we didn't say much. It was more a sort of sitting together in the twilight, a very slow song, well, that's how I felt. No doubt it was different for Elizabeth.

I saw that she was fighting to keep herself under control. She was not crying, but sadness was all over her face. Vince's wife. Vince, the man I loved more than myself, so much more. What I really wanted to do was tell her what a very special husband she had had. And that I knew that better than anyone. A ridiculous thought. What Elizabeth said about Vince was so right and so sweet. As if they had lived close to each other, as if there had been no wrinkles in their love. It didn't sound dramatic, just easy and natural. How she is and once was, so obviously and naturally his wife. Then why was he unfaithful to her, stepping out of their harmonious shared existence?

That tennis racquet on the wall, an old Dunlop Maxply, with one of those clamps around it, a wooden parallelogram, with wingnuts on the four corners. We used to have one at home, and I remember asking my mother if I could remove the clamp. A Maxply, with gut strings, you plucked it with your nails and it made a reassuring sound, everything was fine, the match could begin.

My mother was a good player. Rather than a skirt, she always wore long, cream-coloured trousers. I thought that was interesting, no-one else had trousers like that. I sometimes used to go and watch when she was with her friends on centre court. Sometimes I was the ball girl and I'd roll a ball to her across the court. She'd sweep it up with her racquet in one fluid movement, catch it, throw it into the air, and away the ball would shoot.

I drank my tea, stirred it, it splashed over the edge. I saw the puddle in the saucer, saw once again the kitchen table, where Vince sat floundering. "We have to stop, Maria."

Not those words again. I wanted to go home, to where Maarten was, and I so often was not.

Mustn't stop, keep walking, back to the bus, through the streets, where life is normal. Vince, you can't just slip away like that, we still had so much to talk about. I only read a few sentences, without really knowing what they said. I just saw my name twice.

I think there's a bench in the park I'm about to walk past. I want to have finished reading that letter before I get home. Is it a letter? He wrote Maria on the envelope, and it was sealed. Perhaps that means he wanted to send it. But no, he meant to give it to me this afternoon, of course.

There, the park. With the basketball court, where they're playing a game. Lots of shouting. Good, there's no-one on the bench. I can read it there.

4

Vincent

D.M.,

Sometimes I write down something that happened long ago as if it's happening now. Memories coming treacherously close, trapping me. Old things from the past catching up with me.

In the past, time is no more, someone once said. Time is only past time. Sometimes events slip away from me, I've experienced them, but they don't seem real, they remain distant, fabrications, fragments. And yet they are a part of it too. I don't understand it myself.

And you are a part of everything.

That is why I'm starting a letter to you. We used to write to each other so often. Your small handwriting, you hardly ever crossed out a word, you wrote so much better than I do. This probably isn't going to be like a proper letter. Maybe I'll never send it, or maybe I'll just read a couple of sections to you.

I never wrote to you about Elizabeth, but I think it's allowed after so many years.

It was odd, her complete lack of interest when I said I was going on a trip. I told her I had an appointment with someone that I couldn't get out of, but not for another two weeks. I said something along those lines to her, but I didn't have the impression that she was really listening. She certainly wasn't surprised. It was as if she were somewhere else. We have become those ships that pass in the night. It's not even sad. We're neighbours, we walk through the same rooms and lie under our own sheets with our eyes closed.

I'm sure Elizabeth has someone else. It must be a woman, I saw lipstick on her blouse, and Elizabeth never uses lipstick.

It's still strange to imagine her with a woman. How does that work? Is it very different? I have idyllic images of it. Of a much softer world, everything within reach, so very close to each other. And love not as a task, but as an act of abundance.

Is Elizabeth the same with her as she once was with me? In our prime, without children. Children change everything. They take over your life, disrupting your passion and your love. They cause what blossomed to wither. They put a stop to what was once so thrilling. And you come to love them more than anyone else.

Maybe that is the idyll: woman with woman, no child to drive them apart.

Maria, you're back. All the years without you are forgotten. You said I'd helped you by listening. But I'm sure your story helped me even more.

You gave me Ishmaël's address. It's in a neighbourhood I'd never been to before. A grey hallway, letterboxes bulging with post addressed to people who had presumably moved on. The kind of hallway where farewells hang in the air, a place where you don't want to arrive, only to leave.

No-one knew of an African boy who lived there, never heard of him. There was just one woman who had seen him once. He was small, she said, black jacket and a cap. Yes, but that must have been a year ago. That's the way it works here, she said, no-one ever stays for long, I'm pretty much the only one who's been living here more than two years. It's not a very friendly place.

You told me that Ishmaël always used to go to a sports bar, not far from his home. It was the only clue I had. But there were quite a few of them, sports bars, I mean. I struck it lucky at the fifth one I tried: De Zevensprong, a T.V. screen across the entire width of the place, as if you could step right into the stadium. Silver cups, flags, a faded "Go Ahead" shirt, a vuvuzela, the relics of old tournaments and European Championships and World Cups.

"We are the champions," said a sign above the bar. And the room was full of losers and loners and the lost. No Ishmaël.

But the barman knew him, when I gave him a quick description. Yes, that one, he was a regular for years, sat at the front for every match. Quiet and polite. He spoke to him now and then. Ishmaël was always early. Didn't drink alcohol, only cola.

The last time the barman had seen him was more than a year ago. The boy had shaken his hand and said he was going back.

The barman had asked him where that was, "back".

Freetown, he'd said, I'm going to Freetown.

The barman said he was a sweet kid, but always alone, didn't seem to have any friends. He did cheer though and laugh with the others. Was that his name? Ishmaël?

This is turning into a curious letter. I'm just scribbling down whatever comes to mind, all mixed up together. I'm doing it so that I can tell you later everything that happened when I was looking for him. I think you only half-believed I'd actually go and look for him. However, wherever.

I have no idea what should be the next step.

I'm on the plane to Sierra Leone. Spur of the moment, in search of a needle in a haystack. I remember the look of surprise I gave you when you told me you had been to Sierra Leone. I thought it was rash. And now I'm doing the same. I didn't go to Florence, that friend of mine cancelled his trip, but to Rome. Then I took this plane from Rome. Economy, packed, twice a week to Freetown. There are indistinct figures sitting around me, sunglasses, a few backpackers, women with children.

In business class, men in suits, most of them have taken off their jackets, loosened their ties around those wide white collars, hunched over laptops. What kind of business do they have in Freetown?

Wherever there is chaos, there is business. Wherever there is deprivation, there is business. The strange laws of the jungle.

In the middle of a war, there is trade. War is trade. Men in suits with the wrong shoes and ugly ties and their ever-present laptops, they're the dung beetles of the human world.

I'm sure you think the same, Maria. I wish you had come with me. I'm exaggerating, I know, those people behind the business-class curtain, which is now closed, may well have good intentions, perhaps there are useful calculations on their computers, building plans by some idealistic architect. I'm ranting at nothing, I just wish you were here beside me. I didn't tell you. Or you would have stopped me.

A plane to Freetown. It's a leap into the past, to you, Maria.

"Cabin crew, prepare for landing." I must have dropped off, the sun has gone down, and there's serious turbulence. It seems there's a storm here. More from me tonight or tomorrow.

Freetown by night, it sounds appealing enough when you read about it in the in-flight magazine, the nightclubs, the hotels, the dance parties – people are dancing again, fifteen years after the nightmare. I don't believe a word of it. An editor of the magazine made it all up, or dreamed it. It sounded pretty convincing, but Freetown by night? Just make sure you don't end up there. Cheap brothels, neon light and second-rate whisky in squalid bars, hotels that lock their doors at eleven and roll down the steel shutters. That's how the passenger next to me described the centre.

I arrived in a sweltering, noisy, dusty city, disoriented by the flight and even more so by my own agitation and indecision. Within a few days, you can find your way around a little, but when I'd just got there, I had no idea where to go, except that I needed to find the best hotel to hole up in.

At the airport, they had recommended the Hotel Excelsior, expensive, but fairly safe.

"No legionella," said the girl from something approximating to a tourist office.

The Excelsior was in the centre, not far from the harbour, an old and somewhat disfigured hotel, beautiful but ramshackle inside. Like stepping into the nineteenth century. A dim shadow of antiques, furniture that had never been dusted, and framed photographs of hunting scenes and portraits of Englishmen with big moustaches. A heavy oak staircase to the first floor splits the huge lobby in two. One or two steps are missing.

It was almost night when I arrived. There were still a few people sitting at a couple of tables, Europeans by the look of them. Fans on the ceiling turning slowly, it was a little less stuffy than outside. I was so tired that I just collapsed. And slept dreamlessly until the morning.

Maria, I never told you about Irene. I didn't dare. I thought it was sentimental and I'm sure it would have annoyed you. You're a lot like her. She was my first real love. I was twenty-five, so was she. And a little more than twenty-five years later, I had the same indescribable feelings for you, the same panic when I imagined that one day you would no longer be there.

When I saw you on that boat, I thought just one thing: Irene. Your expressions, your voice, some gestures, your quick remarks, eerily similar. And much later, in your arms, I struggled not to say her name. She had been dead ten years by then, a life with Elizabeth had already intervened. But time does not always outweigh love.

And, believe it or not, sitting at a breakfast table in the hotel there was a woman I remembered seeing and briefly speaking to at Irene's funeral.

As I walked into the dining room, she raised her hand. I almost looked round to see who she was waving at, but then realised it was me. I didn't recognise her, but she knew me because I was one of the people who had spoken at the grave-side. In a cold and windy cemetery where the words were scattered before they could reach anyone.

She had a good memory, though, because she even remembered my name. Invited me to sit with her. I could hardly say no, and I mumbled something about what an amazing coincidence it was. But she hardly seemed surprised at all. Over the years, she said, she'd met lots of people from home. The most recent one was an old classmate who had come breezing into the hotel.

"You meet Dutch people everywhere," she said cheerfully, deciding to settle in for a good chat with me. And that's what happened. A nice woman, curious, alert and tactful. She asked and I answered. She went on asking and I kept on talking.

Sometimes it's easier to tell your story to someone you will most likely never see again. You're less on your guard.

It turned out that this Ellen, that was her name, had worked as young doctor at the hospital where Irene was treated and eventually admitted. They had often spoken, she said she was one of those patients you almost become friends with. Then Ellen had gone and worked for Médecins Sans Frontières. She had been staying at and around the Excelsior for about six months. She organises help for child soldiers who have nowhere to go. Pariahs from a civil war that never ends.

We sat for half the morning at her breakfast table, which eventually turned into a lunch table. She happened to have the day off.

I never told you about the months Irene and I spent travelling through Africa from north to south either. When you started talking about your trip and about my thinking Rome was far enough, I really should have told you I had been there. But then the conversation would have been about me, not you.

Ellen asked me how Irene and I had met. And it was probably because we were in Freetown, but I started telling her that Irene and I had travelled in Africa for three months. All grist to Ellen's mill. She asked me about our journey, and when I stopped talking, she asked more questions.

And off I set again – from Cairo to Cape Town.

Here's the strange thing, Maria. I was talking almost non-stop, and Irene felt close, she sat at the table with us. But gradually she disappeared. Our history evaporated. It became a collection of words, increasingly empty, increasingly unreal. The more details, the more images and anecdotes, the less precise it all became. By the end, she was gone, dissolved. She'll be back though. I have no doubt.

Ellen didn't notice any of this, of course, just listened in fascination, followed our trail, and she was sorry when I finished.

Why was I in Freetown, she asked at last. For some reason, we hadn't spoken about that at all.

I'm looking for a man called Ishmaël Bah, I said.

I wonder if he's in our files.

No, I said, I don't think so. I don't believe he was a child soldier, more likely a victim of child soldiers. Although of course I didn't know that for sure, Maria. Do you?

Child against child. You wonder how they can ever go on with their lives.

They can though, Ellen said. I deal with them on a daily basis. They're often nice boys, always boys, there are hardly any female child soldiers.

They speak about themselves as though it's about someone else altogether, talking about "he" when they mean "I". Ghost children, ghost soldiers, walking around with two voices inside them.

I try to bring back their memories from before the time they fell into the clutches of the rebels or other criminals. Bit by bit it works, very tentatively a space develops for them to touch upon that time, to think about their mothers, a feeling of the past, from before the violence.

A feeling of the past – what is it with us, Maria? You live and you live and the bond that once held you together, where it was timeless, becomes increasingly loose. It's called development – and it's all about unfurling, unveiling. I finally understand that word after so many years as a psychologist. It took a while.

What they call development in my professional circles is an aggressive form of stripping off, becoming increasingly naked, maybe colder, sometimes unhappier. But that is inevitably what happens, with everyone. Everyone loses that feeling of the past, everyone leaves their childhood room, their home and their mother. And many people still long for those things, for something that is no longer there, for a past that has since lost all its magic, for an illusion, a lost time.

Am I talking nonsense? Is there still a point to what I am saying? Perhaps it's because of that conversation with Ellen. I think she's a rather special person, the way she works there, so fearless and energetic, supporting those former child soldiers and ignoring all the cynicism and pessimism around her. She left the Netherlands behind to become a committed relief worker, a practical psychologist for whom a suburban practice with comfy chairs holds no appeal.

*

A week in Freetown, an eternity.

Ellen gave me the name of someone who worked at the Tribunal, maybe they could help me to find out something about Ishmaël. I went there, on the off chance. The Tribunal is over and done with, but there's an archivist who works at the Peace Museum next to the Tribunal building. A museum for peace, as if it's something from long ago, something you have to put on display, so that it won't be forgotten.

The archivist manages all the documents of the Special Court, all the reports and testimonies and recorded crimes. The names of thousands of people who were summoned and interrogated and never prosecuted, and of witnesses and next of kin.

Did he have an Ishmaël Bah on one of his lists?

Yes, more than twenty-five Bahs. One was listed with a note: "presumably departed for the Netherlands". Departed? That no doubt means fled in fear of his life. I asked if his place of birth was known. Yes, a village on the Moa River. It had to be him. Ah, but there was no point going there, as that village no longer existed.

No longer existed? I didn't understand what he was saying.

The Moa had recently flooded its banks, the villagers had just managed to escape the water, but everything had been washed away, not a single house was left standing. Fewer than sixty people had lived there, and they would find somewhere else to live. So that was just a month after you were there!

Most of them were now in temporary accommodation in

Freetown, thanks to the tireless assistance of a doctor who happened to be working in the area at the time.

In Foulah Town, in the hills of Freetown, a tent camp had been set up for a few hundred affected families, all from flooded villages in the Moa region. Near the old mosque, couldn't miss it, everyone knew it.

The man suggested I should visit the camp and ask around. Maybe some of his family members were there, or maybe even the boy himself.

I hesitated, I couldn't imagine that among all those people I'd be able to identify a boy whose face I didn't know, a boy in a black jacket and a baseball cap.

But I did go. It was raining, the kind of rain you see in the movies, blasting down vertically, almost warm water, which just kept on pouring. The call to prayer came from the mosque, with the metallic sound of an inexorable command. I hid under the sheet-iron roof of a bus shelter, although it didn't look as if a bus ever stopped there. The camp was nearby, but I hardly saw anyone, everyone must have been kneeling on the floor. I wondered if the women prayed the same way, it's only ever the men that you picture prostrating themselves.

How in Allah's name was I supposed to find Ishmaël Bah? A pointless trip to this remote spot. Why would he be there? What was I even doing in Freetown, in this torrential rain, in the shadow of a mosque?

Was Ishmaël Muslim? Now I remember you telling me that he observed Ramadan and that he always looked exhausted in the weeks after it. His father would have been Muslim, I think, and his mother Christian. That means you can use religion like a kind of coat that you put on and take off. Ramadan? Christmas? You can participate in both. Religion against the rain, against misfortune, against other people, there's a God for everything in Africa, or so it seems. I sat thinking something along those lines in that bus shelter, in the din of a downpour.

As quickly as the rain came, it was gone. I set off for the camp, along a road that was more like a stream, with just a few patches of mud surfacing from the puddles here and there.

June is an abominable time in Sierra Leone. Sweltering and with constant rain. The runways at Freetown Airport are often flooded.

I spoke to an old man who was pottering round near the entrance to the camp, and, surprisingly, he knew exactly who I meant by Ishmaël Bah, from Holland. He spoke English, had served under the English, he told me. Ishmaël Bah, oh yes, he'd turned up a few weeks back, lived somewhere with a family with lots of children. He'd go and see if he could find him. Wait over there, sir, then you'll be dry. He pointed at a chair under a tarpaulin, where he had himself apparently been sitting. Watching the rain fall, a full-time job.

I waited, unable to think of anything. I just hoped the man

133

wasn't mistaken, that he would not come back with a different boy. Ishmaël Bah, Holland, yes, it could be him.

Then I saw them. The old man and a boy, black jacket, gym shoes, baseball cap. They were walking side by side, slowly, the boy uncertain, the old man unsteady on his feet.

They stopped by the tent, and I stood up. The boy looked at me, took his cap off for a moment, ran his hand over his smooth head and put his cap back on.

I said my name. And then your name, and that I was looking for him on your behalf, and that you'd been waiting for him for a year and didn't know where he was. I said it in Dutch.

And at that same moment I realised that it wasn't him, that it couldn't be him.

He looked at me expectantly, a little surprised, almost indignant. Then he shrugged, asked the old guy something. I didn't understand what he said, of course. The man smiled at me, said he'd got it wrong. That this Ishmaël had never left the country.

Holland, yes, that was the country where the boy was desperate to go, a cousin of his lived there. The old man had heard him talking about Holland a few times recently, that was why. A beautiful country, sir, flowers everywhere. Yes, there must be thousands of people from Sierra Leone living in your country. They have a good life.

But he didn't know how he was going to get there, he had no money and no passport. And that won't get you anywhere.

Do you have any suggestions for him, sir?

The boy slowly looked away, took off his hat again, put it back on. Disappointment gaining the upper hand, he turned around. Shouted something and ran away, back into the camp.

So, Maria, I didn't find him. I promised you, but it didn't work out. The old man stood there beside me, indifferent. He stayed very calm, laid a hand on my shoulder, and we looked in the direction that Ishmaël had run.

Eventually, I thanked the man. He took both of my hands in his, shook his head, said something in a language I didn't know, and then added: God bless you.

Most of it takes place inside our heads, Maria. The wildest things never happen. The most radical, beautiful and daring things, they're mostly in our minds, or we feel it in our bodies, around our hearts. The war is far away, you can go out on the streets, no need to hide anywhere. We just keep a bit of an eye on the situation, so that nothing gets out of hand, that's something we need to prevent.

In so many dreams, I have lived and travelled with you. We lived in houses we could never have. I was often back with my father and mother, restored and young and infinitely happy. All of it in my mind, air, all thin and vague and formless. We float. And we barely know where we are going. Do you know, Maria?

You are looking for Ishmaël, I am looking for you, which is why I looked for Ishmaël. By finding nothing, I think I've lost you for good. If so, I have no idea how I'll go on.

But I'll see you next week.

I feel strangely relieved, Maria. There's a big group of tourists sitting around me, all with blue cords around their necks. They're not going to get lost. With smartphones at the ready, rucksacks and hats, e-readers, bottles, little cushions and blankets, long lines of deeply contented people all heading home. I am one of them. For inexplicable reasons, deeply contented. I can't understand where that sense of detachment comes from. I'm going home, first to Rome, then to Schiphol.

After that, I don't know. I've been wanting to leave for years, to go to another house in another town. I haven't had my practice for a long time now. The children have gone their own ways. I don't see much of them. Elizabeth has changed, but you're still the same and you'll remain the same, no matter where I am. How long do I have to live? I'm sixty-four, maybe ten years, twenty, twenty-five, then I'll have eaten my last potatoes, as I once heard someone say.

These past few years, I had become a mystery to myself, I don't know why, but it's starting to brighten up inside me. I would never dare to claim something like that with anyone listening. But that's how it is. In my plane seat, arm to arm with some tourist in shorts, and with my knees shoved into the seat in front, it is slowly becoming clear.

"The rains that hung between us, Claudien, are over and the night is white." Do you remember that, Maria? A sentence that feels as if it was written for me. Replace Claudien's name with yours, and it's perfect. I know the poet who wrote it, you quoted him a few times. Back then it didn't mean much to me, but I know your poets now. I'm sure you'll be pleased. I was the ideal student without your realising it.

I'm coming back without Ishmaël, and having failed to find out anything about him. I don't think he's in Freetown, but you can never know for certain.

We're about to land, the city's there in the distance.

I'll see you in a few days. I'd love to take you to Rome some time.

5

Maria

What's that they're shouting, those boys? "Under the bench, under the bench!"

They're asking me to throw their ball back. A black boy puts his thumb up at me, and I notice all his friends are black too, all wearing caps. They're fast, jumping up with their ball as if it's no effort at all.

I never thought you'd be able to find Ishmaël, Vince. But you seemed convinced that you would succeed, and I didn't want to discourage you.

You went such a long way for me, I can hardly believe you were really in Freetown. But you must have been, you describe the Excelsior exactly as it is, I went inside it once.

I picture you standing there, with that old man. You seemed so close, didn't you? You thought you had found him. So did I, as I was reading your letter, you wrote your way towards him. Was it a cousin, a brother, a friend of his?

There's no need now, Vince, you did all you could. It doesn't matter that you didn't find him. You didn't succeed, I didn't succeed, and now there's no need.

*

What time is it? I have to stand up, go and catch the bus. The court is empty, those basketball boys had to eat, of course. Everyone's at home now. Probably Maarten too.

Irene. You could have told me about that woman. You didn't dare, that's what you wrote, but I really wouldn't have been jealous of your past. That would be foolish, pointless. But when I confessed to you that I'd been to Africa, you could have told me that you'd spent months travelling there.

You were scared I wouldn't want to be like someone else. And it's true, no-one really wants that, you want to be unique, not to have some sort of doppelganger. Was I Irene? Was I some derivative form of her? I don't believe I was. We had no role models. I never sensed any hidden agenda with you.

I've been sitting here almost an hour. I really should get going, Maarten will be worried.

"Back at half-past six," I wrote in my note to him. He gets anxious if I'm a quarter of an hour later home than I said I would be. When it becomes half an hour, he starts thinking about the police. Now I'm an hour late and my mobile is on my desk. He'll have noticed that already, he must have tried calling me.

Maarten, I'm coming home, I really am coming back to you. You don't need to worry that I'll leave you one day. I know you sometimes think that, I know your fears. A few times, I was on the point of moving out to live alone, but it never lasted, it was just a whim.

Vince is dead.

Maarten hardly knew anything about him. There was no need, he had nothing to do with it, and it certainly doesn't matter now. He tried to track down Ishmaël for me, for us. Maarten would have been so happy if he had found him.

What is it with Maarten and me? I love him, and he loves me, but that doesn't seem enough, and yet it does. Our love is becoming slower, more absent. I sometimes see him standing in the garden, hands in his pockets, his hair greyer when the sun falls on it. There's something defeated about him, melancholy, a fearful suspicion that there is no place left for him in our shared life. I don't know if what I'm thinking is right in any way. Is he worried about getting ill? Is it death that's starting to concern him?

Since Ishmaël left, he has looked older.

These past few months, I've been far too focused on myself. I've been neglecting the house. And Maarten.

So many years with Vince, so many years with Ishmaël, so little time for him.

Vince is dead, Ishmaël missing, nowhere to be found. I don't understand why I'm so calm. It seems as if, in spite of everything, a balance is slowly being restored within me, as if I can think again. I'm at a loss without Vince and without Ishmaël, but I do not feel uprooted. Something seems to be buoying me up, and that's a curious feeling.

*

Not thinking is not a solution. I tried that for a long time. For years, I had to imagine Maarten wasn't there, turning infidelity into fidelity, and chaos into love. With Vince, I lived far above my station, close to heaven. With Maarten in a simple house with lots of rooms where we rarely run into each other. It was easy enough, he was there, he never doubted me, for unfathomable reasons he loved me. At least I was never able to fathom them: why did he pin his hopes on me of all people?

Come on, stand up. Ow, my leg's gone to sleep. It must be this rock-hard bench. It's as if everything in me is asleep, everything seems numb, it's hard to move. There's no strength left in that leg. Stand up first, let it fall. A leg that's gone to sleep, a dead weight, a part of you is no longer there.

Very carefully now, steady. It's quiet on the streets, everyone really does seem to have gone inside.

That letter from Vince, it's as if he had a premonition. Can you perhaps see your own death when it's waiting round the corner? Did he know? Did he even want it?

No, he wanted to go to Rome with me. And certainly not to be buried. I'm with you in Rome, Vince, I'll come and visit, in a year or two. I'll talk to you sometimes, like now: *Mi yidi ma.*

There's the bus. Look, geese flying over the river. In the evening light, they're so surreally beautiful and so without meaning. Those geese denote nothing, they fly, reflect the sky,

I've always found them irresistible. Geese on their way north or south, in constant conversation with one another.

Vince is dead, Ishmaël is nowhere, and I am sitting on a bus, dreaming about geese. It's just as well I wasn't at Vince's funeral. I didn't belong there. I wasn't part of his everyday life, with his family and friends and wife and children. I'd have wanted to speak at the funeral and I'd have started crying. No-one would have understood.

Maarten will have gone round to the neighbours by now to ask if they know where I am.

I have to get off the bus now. I have to go home.

There he is, by the gate.

Maarten, I'm close. I'm walking in the shadow of the trees. I'm walking to you, and you're looking the other way. You don't know it yet, but I'm almost home.

OTTO DE KAT is the pen name of Dutch publisher, novelist, poet and critic Jan Geurt Gaarlandt. His award-winning novels have been widely published in Europe.

LAURA WATKINSON is a translator from Dutch, Italian and German whose translations include works by Cees Nooteboom, Jan van Mersbergen, Tonke Dragt and Peter Terrin.